D1095085

ROUGH TRADE

Lou Rand

ROUGH TRADE

ARGYLE BOOKS
Los Angeles, California

ROUGH TRADE

CHAPTER ONE

Hattie Campbell—gray, angular, and efficiently smart—always arrived at the office early. Today in particular she felt that she must be on hand. A new owner, Mr. Francis Morley, was to take over actual charge. While the efficient Miss Campbell had been assured that she would have a place as long as there was an agency, she had an intuitive idea that her private preserve of many orderly years was about to be disrupted.

This new man, old Harry's nephew, had been in and out several times the previous day but the opportunity she had sought for a good, long get-acquainted talk had just not materialized. Hattie hadn't quite made up her mind whether she liked the young man anyway. After many years as an employee, and later office manager of a detective agency, she was well aware of the 'facts of life'. And in Bay City, home of the Arts, culture, bohemianism, and all of the several things that were meant by this last term—things mentioned only in joking—she knew only too well that the simple old classification of 'men and women' simply didn't cover the situation any longer.

About Francis Morley, she was puzzled. The guy had charm, manners, and a certain bubbling exuberance, but he was certainly not the man old Harry Morley had been. And who should know better than Hattie? For thirty years she had been secretary, assistant, mother, companion—everything in fact, that she could be to Francis Morley's uncle.

There had never been any question of romance for them, but a healthy respect and need for each other instead. The idea of marriage had really never entered their minds. Hattie, at nearly sixty, had been hard hit at Harry's passing, but at his request had kept the old agency going. She had finally located the nephew. Now, she supposed, she could retire. Harry had left her secure. But she felt strongly that she should stick around for awhile and help Francis get started.

These last few days she wasn't so sure; this nephew was definitely a character. Sort of on the swish side too, she thought. But maybe that was only the 'theatre' that had rubbed off on him. She hoped so, because he really

10

did seem to be a nice person, if just a little too pretty for her tastes.

Well, Hattie mused to herself while going up in the elevator, the man had said that he would be down early today and start taking over. Also, he'd said something about putting an ad in the papers for a steady assistant, and then going after some more business. Thank goodness! she mentally conceded.

The old standby accounts were paying the rent. But she agreed that a few new clients would help. She was really happy that Francis had definitely said the agency would do no divorce work. In this he was following Harry's ideas. Harry had believed steadfastly in the inviolable privacy of married people.

Then, too, Francis had said something about decorators. He'd really been pretty vague about this, as she thought of it now. Hattie realized that most of her new employer's conversations to date had been definitely on the vague side.

"Oh, hell!" she said softly to herself as she stepped out of the elevator, "it'll all work out . . ."

As she rounded the corner of the hallway leading to the agency offices, she was brought to an abrupt halt by the line of men stemming from the agency door. They were six-deep, waiting patiently in front of the door bearing the inscription: "MORLEY AGENCY—PRIVATE INVESTIGATIONS".

Why! she thought, dumbfounded, there must be dozens of them!

The air was filled with the leavening smoke of half

11

a hundred cigarettes, but there seemed to be little conversation. Most of the men carried a morning paper. Hattie realized at once that Francis must have put that advertisement in the paper. Humph! An assistant, no less. And from the want ads!

Sniffing audibly and squaring her adequate shoulders in her smart suit, Hattie pushed her way through to the door behind which she could hear the phone ringing. The men near the door grudgingly gave way, allowed her to open it and step inside.

As they started to push in behind her, Hattie, instinctively feeling the need for a little preparation for the coming onslaught, turned and announced in very positive tones that the office would not be opened for at least another half hour. Disregarding another forward surge and an unpleasant murmur from the mob, she managed to get the door closed again, and she bolted it from the inside.

Darting to her desk, she dumped her purse, paper, and a copy of a late novel. Then she snatched at the jangling telephone. To an earnest inquiry about the 'ad', she briskly replied that Mr. Morley would only interview in person and hung up. The instrument rang again at once, with an almost identical interchange as a result.

This continued for several minutes, until the pattern was broken by someone calling from Duke -and -Dixie's, demanding to know when Mr. Morley would see the samples. This was all a complete mystery to Hattie, but certainly a welcome relief. She promptly suggested that

Mr. Morley would probably look at anything at ten o'clock. This time, the other party hung up first.

At this, Hattie simply took the receiver off the hook, and quickly fumbled open her morning paper. An ominous series of knocks and raps on the outer door had begun to add to the bedlam of the morning. The secretary of the Morley Agency thought that she had better get a look at the 'ad' before going any further. Skimming through the extensive want ad section, she came almost at once to the notice over the more heavily printed name, 'THE MORLEY AGENCY'.

Lighting a cigarette for strength, she slowly and carefully read what was printed there, wincing at each succeeding line:

YOUNG MAN WANTED—Rough, tough, attractive; 25-30; 6 ft or over; educated, ex-service office preferred. 'Man-of-the World' type, single, unattached, familiar with weapons. Must be bondable for permanent employment as assistant to private investigator. Excellent salary plus private apartment. Good future to right party.
THE MORLEY AGENCY.

Lifting her eyes to the ceiling in silent prayer, Hattie could only murmur, "oh, brother", as she wearily put the phone back on its hook. It rang immediately.

At this moment, just down the hall, Francis Morley stepped jauntily from the elevator. Slightly over medium height, he appeared to be slender; but this slimness could be deceiving. More or less violently extreme sports clothes carried upwards the note set by the open sandals. He wore his hair in overlong but nicely waved blond curls.

Francis Morley's features were fine, aristocratic, and just a shade too regular. An unconsciously un-masculine air was hinted at by the play of brilliant blue eyes beneath his long, luxuriant lashes. The wide and handsome Morley brow was at the moment a bit pale, an indication of a slightly hung-over condition. As he paced lissomely down the hall and approached the Agency door, he pondered briefly on this gay, gay city that offered so many opportunities for companionship. Shouldn't have done it last night, he mused, this being the first day at the Agency and all.

His line of thought was shattered as he turned the corner of the hall. The Agency was surrounded by dozens of restive men. All ages were here; young, old, fair and fat, well-dressed and otherwise. In a flash Francis realized that they had all come in answer to his ad, and were all probably waiting for him. Drawing himself up, he wedged his way through to the door, pausing only to give a haughty backward glance to some character who gave a low whistle. Fumbling out his key, he got it into the lock. As he opened the door, he turned to face the crowd:

"I'm Mr. Morley. Now if you fellows will come in five or six at a time, I'll see you all as quickly as possible."

With a gay lift to his shoulders, he turned to face Hattie at her desk.

14

"My God, Bessie! It looks like the third act of Aida out there!"

"Why didn't you tell me?" replied his secretary. "We could've had an agency weed out the applicants".

Since ten men had crowded into the reception room behind him, Francis fled into his private office, motioning Hattie to join him. Inside, with the door closed, Francis immediately went to the little closet washroom and mixed a hasty Bromo. The elderly secretary waited patiently by his desk.

When he emerged, she smiled encouragingly and asked, "Who are Duke and Dixie?"

"Duke and Dixie? Why?"

"Well, they called and said that they were to see you this morning. I told them ten o'clock".

"Oh, I know. The decorators. I've decided that we should touch up the place a bit."

"You'd better get with the boys outside then." Hattie indicated the outer office. "Your decorators will be here with samples in about an hour."

"Oh no!" Francis almost shrieked. "Hattie, I'm not well this morning."

"Come dear," Hattie laughed, "pull yourself together. The show must go on."

"All right, Agatha. Put Duke and Dixie in the extra office when they get here." He paused as he inspected his well-groomed hands. "I've got a dreadful hangnail," he commented.

"Humph! I feel for you. What about this mob out-

15

side, to say nothing of the telephone going like mad—"

"All right, all right! Never mind the lash. I'll take care of the boys—one at a time, that is—and you get to the phone. Business as usual, dearie . . ."

As Hattie went back to her desk, Francis fitted a cigarette into a long holder, adjusted the window shades to a less penetrating glare, and sank resignedly into the chair behind the desk. Clicking on the interoffice communication, he said in a tired voice,

"Okay. Send 'em in."

CHAPTER TWO

At noon the same day, Captain of Detectives John Starr strode into Flanagan's, a small bar near Bay City's Hall of Justice. He nodded only briefly to the man behind the counter. Without pause, Captain Starr strode the length of the premises and passed through a door at the rear.

The room the detective entered was another milieu entirely. Graciously spacious and fitted out as the lounge of an exclusive gentleman's club, this was the famous 'Back Room'. With several obscure entrances and exits, with a tiny kitchen and a small service bar presided over by an aged and efficient Chinese, the Back Room had been for almost a century the quiet gathering place of many of Bay City's finest citizens. These included judges, lawyers, professional men—and, on occasion, over the years, one or two gentlemen connected with the local police.

The "Back Room crowd" was never a membered group, nor were there such devices as dues and meetings. Those who were welcome came and went as they chose. Others found entrance doors locked, or were simply turned away by the ageless waiter and bartender, Mr. Wong, who was the sole arbiter. It was, nevertheless, a quiet and companionable place. By several unwritten but understood rules, pending cases of judges, lawyers, police, and the business of others who might be present, were not discussed. The news personnel who were admitted seldom quoted anything said or heard here, and then only with express permission.

As Captain Starr entered he was pleasantly greeted by those who sat about the huge central table.

Next to the detective officer, as he seated himself, was Jay Patton, one of the city's leading attorneys, frequently referred to as the 'Old Master'. A quiet appearing and genteel man, one would hardly suspect the number of murderers, embezzlers and other criminals whom he had, temporarily at least, freed from the toils of the law. On the Captain's other hand, was another figure often seen and read about in the local papers—Senator Martin.

Bruce Martin was a distinguished and cultured gentleman. Chairman of many private and public committees, he was surely one of Bay City's most prominent citizens. The Senator was a bachelor. He was past fifty, and was considered to be a man of means. It was also considered that his means had been inherited, for he had no obvious source of income.

The Senator was a quiet, even-tempered but reticent old gentleman. Never a fop, he was definitely a man about town.

Though Captain Starr sat down next to the Senator, the latter seemed hardly to notice his presence, aside from a perfunctory greeting. He was seemingly engrossed in conversation with a rather brash young man, Bert Karl, a columnist of Bay City's leading newspaper.

Bert Karl sounded off daily about local personages, their fads and foibles. Though young, Karl was clever, and his widely read column was often delightfully humorous and interesting. His items were personal but never vicious, as currently seemed to be the fashion with certain braying and crusading columnists in eastern cities. It was to him that Starr addressed himself.

"Bert, what's the latest that the police should know about but probably don't?" he asked with a smile.

Karl had paused in what he had been saying to the Senator, but before he could reply, a heavy laughing voice from across the table cut in on the interchange. The booming voice of Tiger Olsen, a professional football player turned used-car salesman—cut in with:

"Kane's been giving us the lowdown on this guy, or woman, or whatever it is, who went to Denmark and had his marbles removed." Olsen's jolly laughter was infectious and brought out smiles all around the table.

Without letting him finish, the columnist chimed in, "Yeah, but get this for a laugh: At the Council meeting yesterday, the Commissioner started to discuss the suggestion that the city again operate ferries on the Bay. Well, some one loudly remarked that he would like to see more ferries on the Bay and fewer on the streets."

The gentlemen laughed at this story, though the football player evinced a slight disgust at the type of person indicated.

Another of the group, Joe Cannelli, a rather gross, middle-aged man who operated a bar and restaurant, shrugged expressively, and with fair accuracy summed up the local opinion of sexually confused persons:

"Live and let live, I always say."

Kane laughingly put in: "You always say. But my little birdie tells me you've got a new bartender at your joint who's very gay."

Cannelli pretended to be annoyed as he growled, "What the hell. The union sent him. Besides, he's pretty."

Here Captain Starr broke in.

"Let me tell you a real funny story—and it happened only this morning. Do any of you remember the old Morley Agency? Old man Morley was one of the first in the city to have a private license."

The attorney nodded. "I remember. He did some jobs for me once or twice. Very reliable. And a very decent old fellow."

Karl interrupted. "Say, didn't he die just last year?"

"That's the fellow," continued the plain-clothesman, "Now it seems that he had some steady accounts, quite a sizeable business, skip-tracing, and stuff like that. The lawyers who handled his estate have kept the office open. Some old girl—Morley's secretary for thirty years—has been running it, with some extra help now and then. Well, as I get the story, there was only one heir to whatever was left. They finally located him back East, and now he's out here and is going to take over."

"He in the business, too?" queried Olsen.

This brought a short laugh from the police officer. "Well, it all depends on what business you mean. He has 'been in the theater', as he puts it, but it seems to me that he was actually a chorus man in a musical show."

This brought further grins and laughter around the table.

"They say that some of those guys are all man," volunteered the gruff man.

"Not this one," put in Starr. "He came in to get a license and a gun permit. A very pretty fellow with a roving eye. Of course, I could be wrong, but I think . . ."

"Don't tell us that he made a pass at you, Captain," wryly put in the poker-faced Senator, obviously looking over the officer's very regular and very masculine features. This, and the Senator's droll manner, brought more hilarious laughter from the group.

"How about it, Starr? Is it, or isn't it?" asked Olsen.

Pausing speculatively before answering, the Captain said, "Hell, you can't always tell these days. But when I asked this character what he needed a gun for, he just rolled his eyes, put his hand on his hip, tossed back his wavy hair and shrieked at me that he'd have a helluva time beating off some attacker with a mascara brush . . ."

Tiger Olsen joined the laughter this time. "This I have to see," he said.

"Maybe you can sell him a car, is what you mean," jibed Karl.

Tiger nodded. "Right. A bright pink XKE." He got up during the laughter that followed and left the bar.

CHAPTER THREE

By one o'clock, Hattie Campbell was beginning to have a glazed look about the eyes. Between the steadily growing horde of applicants, and the continuous ringing of the phone, she was reaching a point just short of hysteria.

Added to the confusion were several more or less mad inter-office communications. And still the applicants seemed to come and go. The uproar in the outer office was calm and serene, however, in comparison to the scene behind the door marked "Private."

Across the room from Morley's desk, balanced at

the top of a shaky stepladder, was a nondescript person clad in blue dungarees, run down half-Wellingtons, a striped Jersey in pink and green, topped by a wild mop of mottled red hair. This person was holding up lengths of brightly colored draperies in either hand while muttering something unintelligible into the wainscoting. But these efforts actually had only a part of Francis' attention.

Squeezed into another chair behind the desk was a pert blonde manicurist, who was working deftly, though with an air of confusion, on one of Francis' hands. The hangnail, no doubt.

Added to the bright chatter of the blonde, and the mutterings of Duke (or Dixie—one couldn't be sure, really) the applicant seated before the desk began to show signs of increasing nervousness. He had just delivered an idealized description of self and abilities, and had arrived at that conversational pause that requires something from the other party. Francis, who had decided 'NO' at first glance, seemed to be actually more interested in the minor mystery of Dixie (or Duke).

At this point the intercom system brayed forth a frantic plea from Hattie.

"Mr. Morley, are we taking cases this morning?"

"Certainly, my dear. Business as usual." This last with a subdued titter.

"Please, sir, do hold still." This from the manicurist in an affected, lispy, little girl's voice.

The mutter from atop the ladder became a derisive snort, and a heavy voice mimicked: "Please, sir, do hold still.' Get her!"

Right back came the very earthy natural tones of the handholder: "Up ya' bucket, Butch!"

The intercom chimed in again. "A Mrs. Bagnold wants us to find the Emir of Afghanistan—whoever that may be."

"Well for pity sakes, how did she lose him? Say, Hattie, do we trace missing persons?"

"Ya gotta missing link up the tree there," snapped the manicurist, rolling up her tools. "That'll be two-fifty."

Duke (or Dixie) started a hasty descent but became entangled in the yards of her draperies. From the midst of the entanglement came a threatening "Let me at that blondined Navy-bait . . ."

"Ladies! Please!" said Morley.

"She says that that will be satisfactory, and when will you see her?" came from Hattie.

"Yeah! You and who else?" said one of the belligerants.

"What will be satisfactory?" demanded Francis.

"Mr. Morley, there is no need to raise your voice. You said 'two-fifty', and so I told Mrs. Bagnold that we'd be happy to locate the missing Emir—for two hundred and fifty dollars. And she agreed. She will be in this afternoon with the details."

The nervous applicant had begun to squirm, apparently unable to remain a spectator only, he burst forth with a peal of falsetto laughter. Leaning across the desk and patting Francis' arm, he burbled:

"My Gawd, dearie! This is the gayest place in town. I'd just love to work here." Slumping coquettishly over the desk he leered inanely. "And I'll just bet that you and I could find lots in common. . . ."

Repressing a shudder, Francis arose with considerable dignity. "I do not think, sir, that you are just the person. I wanted an ex-officer, someone younger, perhaps."

His meaning was very clear, and the rejected man also rose. Drawing himself up haughtily, he replied in his original curt tones:

"Possibly I was mistaken, Mr. Morley. Certain types always want someone younger. As for myself, I'll have you know that I was a Lieutenant Colonel in the Air Force!"

Turning, he strode to the door with an air of offended dignity. He went out, followed by the manicurist, who winked at Francis in passing, and remarked, "Yah! these fly-boys."

From the ladder, Dixie (or Duke) put in, "Well, Morley, what do you think?"

The fact that she obviously wanted an opinion on the draperies went unnoticed.

The harassed Morley flipped a key and said wearily into the intercom: "Hattie, are there many more?"

"There certainly are, dozens of them! Also, will you see a Mr. Olsen?"

"What does he want?"

"He's with Chadwick Motors. We carry the account. Remember, sir—business as usual!"

Resignedly Francis said, "Send him in."

From the ladder came a more frantic waving of the drapes.

"Well, pal, what do you think?"

"I think I need a rest," the head of Morley Agency said.

The door opened to admit Tiger Olsen. Francis sat up in his chair, immediately interested in this newcomer.

"Well, let's do this quickly, a client is coming in. What was your school?"

The tall, well-dressed and attractively large man smiled and said hesitantly, "Perhaps, Mr. Morley—"

"Please," he snapped, "allow me just a few questions first. Did you take a degree?" Francis looked over the two-hundred-pounds-plus of Olsen's development, noted the erect carriage, the good if slightly disarranged features, the excellent tailoring.

Amused, Tiger decided to play along. "Yes, sir. Arts —'44."

"In Service?"

"Captain, Marine Corps."

"Single?"

"Definitely."

"Well . . ." Approval began to shine in Francis eyes. "Know the City?"

"Born here. Lived here all my life."

"Well, er, one moment." Flipping the intercom, Francis barked: "Hattie, please come in."

The door admitted the secretary almost at once. "Mr. Morley, this phone is driving me mad."

"Never mind that for a moment." Nodding at Tiger, relaxed and grinning in his chair, Francis asked, "What do you think of this one?"

27

"What do you mean?" asked a puzzled Hattie.

"Personally, I think he's just the type."

At this both Tiger and the secretary exchanged amused glances and burst out laughing.

"What the hell is so funny?" demanded Francis.

"Mr. Morley, this is Mr. Olsen—Mr. Tiger Olsen of Chadwick Motors."

Slumping in his seat, Francis moaned, "Oh, no!"

"Oh, but yes . . ." said Hattie. Then she turned to the visitor with something near hero-worship in her eyes. "I remember, Mr. Olsen, when you came back. The parade went by just down below, and I frantically tore up paper and poured it out the window." Turning to Francis, she explained excitedly, "Mr. Olsen was a returned war hero."

From the top of the ladder came: "Say listen, you, never mind all that yak-yak. I can't stay up here all day."

Sizing up the situation, and in all modesty preferring to change the subject, Tiger asked Francis deferentially, "Mr. Morley, in my line I have had quite a lot of experience with custom upholstery. Now, may I make a suggestion here?"

"Why, certainly, please do. And my apologies, Mr. Olsen."

Turning to Dixie (or Duke), Tiger said, "I think that a rough copper drapery with maybe some metal in it would do well in here. Walls and woodwork in shades of light green, possibly some blue in it, but no yellow. The furniture in off-white leather, a darker green broadloom on the floor, bone-white desk, and one or two lamps with copper shades and so on."

"Brother, I wouldn't have believed it possible, but that's darn near perfect. You can come work for me, too, anytime ya' want to. How about it, Morley?"

"It all sounds grand to me. But first bring me in some samples in those colors, and we'll talk about prices. Am I free tomorrow afternoon, Hattie?"

"Not the way that mob out there is showing up."

"About four, then," said Francis to the decorator, who was bundling the draperies and ladder out the door.

"Maybe I can help you a little further," offered Tiger. Turning to Hattie, he said, "Call Helen Roberts at the Preferred Answering Service—use my name—and ask her to monitor your calls, just putting through the actual business calls. Have her ask applicants to write in, giving their details and stuff. I think that she can get the phone company to make the switch in about an hour."

Heaving a sigh of relief, Hattie turned to the door.

"I don't know how I'll ever thank you, Mr. Olsen."

Then Tiger had a further suggestion. "If you would take all the names out there now, and route them back at five minute intervals, starting, say, at two o'clock, well, you could see about twenty every hour."

Overjoyed at this very sensible suggestion, Hattie went out beaming, with Francis' nod of approval.

Tiger turned to the man at the desk and said, "And now, Mr. Morley, if you have a few minutes to spare?"

"Mr. Olsen, you are out of this world! You can have

29

all of my time that you want, but, what was it about?"

"It's like this," Tiger relaxed in his chair, as he went on. "I'd heard that you're new in Bay City, and I thought that perhaps sooner or later you'd be interested in a motor car. Now it appears to me that your business here is likely to be a very distinguished one. So, I don't feel that I'm at all out of line in suggesting that you consider one of our very distinguished cars. Our agency has the privilege of offering—"

At this point, his fine flow of sales-talk was interrupted, as with uplifted hand Francis asked, "Mr. Olsen, in a word, you are a car salesman?"

"That's correct, Mr. Morley."

"If you don't mind the personal note this once—are you happy at it?"

"Well, sir, yes and no. The business has its ups and downs."

"Are you very sure that you wouldn't prefer to work on a steady salary basis, with, say—a year's contract as my assistant?"

"Mr. Morley, this is nice of you. It's a thing that I could consider."

"Mr. Olsen, I'll make you a proposition."

Looking Francis directly in the eyes, Tiger smiled wryly, and said, "That, Mr. Morley, is what I am afraid of."

Francis met the Tiger's glance steadily enough, though he did flush slightly. Then he continued,

"There would be, possibly, some pre-conceived notions, about which I should have to disillusion you. The proposition that I have in mind is that I'll be very happy to purchase a car from you if it is your final sale for Chadwick, just prior to your coming to work for the Morley Agency at your own figure."

Hesitant, and aware of the fact that possibly his casual snap judgment might have made a bit of a fool of himself, Tiger replied, "I'll consider it, Mr. Morley, now about this car."

Jumping to his feet, a more ebullient Francis gayly remarked, "Mr. Olsen, I'm just worn out here, though you seem to have straightened out most of my day for me. I thought perhaps that I would go and take a little refreshing exercise and then lunch. While you are considering my offer and I'm thinking about yours, wouldn't you care to join me?"

Tiger grinned. "That's right, there's nothing like a good workout. I'd be happy to join you. Where do—?"

Anticipating the question, Francis strode to the door. "I've discovered a perfectly divine ballet school, and only a couple of blocks from here."

Tiger blanched. "Did you say 'a ballet school'?"

"Yes, I'm sure you'll love it. And you might be surprised."

The two men left the office. Francis paused at the reception desk to tell Hattie where they were going.

Getting into the elevator, Tiger again shook his head, and muttered, "a ballet school. . . ."

CHAPTER FOUR

After a short drive about the City, during which Tiger Olsen extolled the merits of his own Jaguar sports car in which they rode, Francis' directions brought them to a rather down-at-the-heels building whose most prominent feature was a large and permanent sign, HALLS FOR RENT. At the entrance, a display board listed, among other things, a "Personal" Get-Acquainted Club; Sanhedran's Gymnasium and School of Physical Culture; the Boros Toros Chorus of the Flamenco; and the Marie Antoinette Ballet Academy.

Tiger studied this directory as if seeking a last-minute

reprieve, and finally, reluctantly, followed Francis' foot-steps to the stairway.

" 'You walks'," said Francis, obviously quoting an authority. "That's what they told me." Sizing up the big, athletic figure following him up the stairs, he added, "I'm sure that Sandy will be able to fix you with a costume."

"Well, look, Mr. Morley, maybe some other time—"

"Come on, don't be a chicken."

A resigned Tiger merely nodded his head and plodded on upward.

A dull door in a drab hallway, to which Francis had a key, let them into a small but well appointed locker room. Tiger was a bit surprised at this adjunct to a ballet school, but was by now determined to see this thing through.

"San-n-ndy!" called Francis at the top of his voice. This brought in a wizened little character who looked to Tiger like the handler of a third-rate pug.

"Good morning, Frank, and why, yeah! It's Tiger Olsen." He put out a hand and pumped Olsen's enthusiastically. "We never met, but of course, I seen you around."

Francis interrupted, "This is Sandy. He owns the place. My, but you certainly seem to have contacts, Olsen."

"Yeah. Lots of people know me. Local boy, y'know."

"Sandy, have you got some stuff for Tiger? We want to do a little toe work."

"Sure, sure. Come around here, Tiger."

As he led the big fellow around behind some lockers,

Francis called after him, "Bring him in when he's ready, Sandy."

"You betcha, Frank," called the trainer from an unseen corner.

Five minutes later he led Olsen, now clad in trunks and a T-shirt, into a fairly large gymnasium. Only a couple of men were present. One was working out on some weights in a far corner. And there was a flashy guy who looked to be a light-light-heavy punching a bag rhythmically and expertly. He stopped as Tiger came in.

The man at the bag, looking a bit top-heavy in his well padded head and face protector, turned and came toward Tiger and Sandy, stopping to pick up another fighter's mask on his way.

"You're pretty good with that bag this morning, Frank," Sandy said. "Now, what's it gonna be with the Tiger?" Unaware of the big man's dumfounded confusion, the little trainer talked on as he led Tiger over to the padded ring. "Tiger's got about fifty pounds on you, Frank, but he looks—you'll excuse it, please, Tiger—he looks a little fat here and there."

"That's what I thought, too," said Francis, "and a little musclebound. And besides, I've got a hunch that he can't box."

The embarrassed Olsen climbed after the others into the ring. At Morley's insistence he donned the protective headgear, while explaining that he had sparred around a little in college—but really hadn't done much boxing.

"Okay, Tiger, this is just for the exercise," said the amused Francis. "Let's try a couple of two minute rounds.

34

Time us, will you, Sandy? And listen, big man, I'm not expecting, so let's get it in there."

One and two-thirds minutes later, a bewildered ex-football player and all-around athlete looked up from where he sat in the center of the ring. He growled a bit truculently, "Kinda rough, aren't you, chum?"

"That, Mr. Olsen, was to knock one idea out of your mind."

Getting to his feet and shaking his head, Olsen admitted, "Well, boy, that you did, and for sure. Why?"

Morley cut him short, "Aw, come on, slugger. Get in there and box. We both need the workout. Then, maybe, we'll go get that new car of mine."

An hour or so later, in the offices of the Chadwick Motor Company, Francis passed over his check and received the pink slip that denoted his ownership of the snappy, underslung Jaguar at the curb. Smiling, the sales manager patted Tiger lightly on the shoulder.

"Nice work, boy." At Francis' amused chuckle, the manager explained "Not many get 'em with the full price in cash these days."

Francis grinned wickedly, "Yes, I'm sure that you'll miss Mr. Olsen."

The Tiger cut in, embarrassed, feeling that this should come from him.

"Sir, I hope that there won't be any hard feelings about this, but Mr. Morley has convinced me—that is, he has asked me to join his Agency as his assistant. And, well, I've agreed."

35

"Now look here, Olsen, if it's a question of more money—"

"No, no, sir. That's not it. It's just that I'm thinking that the work will be more interesting. Besides, the car business isn't too good right now . . . and, well, sir, you know how it is."

Resignedly, the manager admitted that he did know how it was, though in his own mind, after a hasty appraisal of the two men, he was not entirely sure that he did. After some further conversation, Francis and Tiger were again out on the sidewalk.

"I think you'd better go down to the police department first thing tomorrow and get a license, or whatever, Tiger. And while we're on the subject, you'd better call me Frank, when you feel friendly."

"Okay, boss. I'll go down and see Captain Starr, and then see you back at the office at ten tomorrow morning."

Francis laughed. "Will Hattie be surprised!" All those guys in this morning, and for nothing."

"Yeah, you'd better phone her and have her put a notice on the outside door that the position has been filled. And, say have her call Helen Roberts at the phone service, too."

Francis laughed again, and mincing a bit toward his new car, said, "Oh I can see that you're going to be a big help to me. By the way," he paused, "I've already got a case for you."

"Yeah?" Tiger seemed a bit apprehensive.

"Yeah!" Francis said, "Butch, we've got to locate

the Emir of Afghanistan for Mrs. Bagnold by five o'clock tomorrow afternoon. So there, you great hulk. Now get moving."

Glancing around to be sure they were unobserved, Tiger put a hand on his hip and flipped his other wrist.

"And whoops to you, too," he said with his boyish grin.

CHAPTER FIVE

Several blocks from the Morley Agency, a fog-swept park stretched for blocks and blocks, westward through the heart of Bay City and on to the cold, tide-washed, shore of the ocean. Behind the beach and all about the park, Bay City was sleeping—or almost all of it.

A fast sedan roared past the building which housed the Morley Agency, pulled off the highway from the park and shuddered to a jerking halt as it lost traction in the sand. The front doors opened on either side and two men got out. The driver was the younger, well dressed in casual sports clothes. Of average height and weight, he carried himself with a noticeably peculiar hauteur, and walked with a short, mincing step—almost that of a dancer or a model. As he moved toward the front of the sedan, his bigger and burlier companion snapped at him in a brusque tone.

"Goddam it, Kay—turn off the lights!"

This man was older than the other. He was also handsome, in a brutish, appealing sort of way. His attire was also casual, but his manner was nervous. Across his heavy forehead, above beetling, coarse brows, were beads of perspiration. His strong mascular hands clenched and unfolded aimlessly.

The driver did not seem to notice this tension. He switched off the car's lights and joined his companion. His voice, suited to his figure, was peculiarly light and lilting for a man. It came with a giggle:

"Well, Buster, want another crack at him? or would you go for something a little more lively?"

Almost fiercely the bigger man turned on the other.

"Shut up, Kay! Let's get this done with . . ."

Turning to the rear of the automobile, the big man opened the door and reached into the back of the car. A moment later he heaved a body out on to the sand.

The head of this inert figure was wrapped with a soiled towel; the body was dressed in a dark suit, with black shoes. Both men stood hesitantly over the muffled corpse. After a moment's silence, the smaller remarked rather plaintively, "Why isn't there more blood?"

Almost savagely the other replied, "The hell with that! Take his feet. We'll get him down to the water."

39

The smaller of the two stiffened and shuddered, and struck a disdainful pose. His lower lip trembled, and his hands fluttered from limp wrists.

"But, Buster . . ." he began.

"But Hell! You silly bitch, this is murder. We gotta get him down to the water without leaving any tracks, like if we dragged him. If I carried him, I'd get all bloo . . . well, messed up. So we both gotta do it. Now, goddam you, Kay, pick up his feet."

Buster picked up the shoulders of the body and Kay reluctantly lifted the feet. Down to the water's edge, they trudged crabwise with their bulky burden, which they dropped at the break of the surf.

A spent wave came in and washed tiredly up the sloping sand. Kay danced nimbly out of it's path. Buster reached down and removed the towel from the head of the corpse. The bloodied, battered features stared up sightlessly, and a few locks of abundant hair flowed gently back with the receding water. The heavy man turned and strode up the beach to the waiting car, the other swiftly behind him, as if afraid to be left alone with the corpse they had just discarded. Only once did Kay pause. Turning, with a backward flip of his expressive wrist, he said in a voice that was gayly affected, but quavering, "Well! She'll get her bath tonight, hey, Buster?"

As the two reached the car, Buster turned to glare speculatively at the other. Kay, now seemingly in a different mood, paused beside the bigger man. With his head thrown back, his throat arched coquettishly, and his eyelids fluttering, Kay seemed almost feminine. Putting

40

his hand gently and caressingly on his companion's muscular arm, he said petulantly, "You promised, Buster, if I'd help."

After a moment's hesitation, the big man replied roughly: "Okay. Why not? But—let's be quick."

Both men climbed into the spacious rear of the sedan and closed the door.

There was a high gasp of delight from within the dark cave of the back seat. A rustling sound followed and the gasp turned into a low moan of pleasure. The big sedan began to rock rhythmically on its springs. Heavy breathing and excited groans drifted out of the open windows.

The car tilted gayly back and forth in a final frenzy and then all was silent. Several minutes passed. Then, the rear doors opened and the two men resumed their places in the front seat. The engine roared to life and the car sped back along the parkway. It took a sideroad, winding upward, and finally came to rest once more beside a small park at the top of one of the city's hills. It remained parked for a few minutes, squatting ominously without lights, when another car pulled up across the street. After a moment a man got out of this second car and, looking nervously around at the dark, deserted neighborhood, walked across to the big sedan. As he approached, a rear door swung open and Kay's lisping voice said,

"Come on. Get in."

Almost reluctantly, the man climbed into the back seat of the big car.

Kay tersely demanded, "Did you bring it?"

41

"Now listen, Kay, this is a lot of money. I had to borrow—"

"Okay! Cut the crap, dearie. You had your fun, now you've got to pay for it. Give it to me."

"Well, first you give me the pictures, and the negatives, too!"

Kay laughed bitterly. "Not this time. Come on, hand over the money.

"What do you mean, 'not this time'?"

"I mean that this is only the first installment, and if you don't make your payments promptly, that invalid sister of yours and that boss of yours will each get a copy of that picture. Though, I can't say that they really do me justice."

The man started to protest angrily, and reached for the handle of the door to let himself out of the car. At this the hulking figure sitting in the driver's seat turned, quietly levelling a snubnosed automatic at the frantic man behind.

"Get the money, Kay!" snapped Buster.

The protesting man leaned well forward, closer to the one in front, as if to plead personally with him. Before he could say a word, Buster's other hand reached high, and the descending gun butt hit the pleader expertly just behind the ear. He slumped limply forward.

"Come on now, Kay. Get the money and hand it over."

The young blond man fumbled through the pockets of the unconscious man. Finally, he sat up, holding a thick envelope. After making sure that this contained currency, he leaned forward to pass it to his companion in the front seat.

Taking the money, Buster said, "Let's get him out of here. We'll drag him over on to the grass."

The two carried the man over into the park and dumped him limply beside some bushes. Kay gayly remarked, "My God, we always seem to be trundling bodies . . ."

The lissome youth bent to remove the unconscious man's wallet. As he started to rise with it in his hand, Buster shot him neatly between the eyes.

Moving swiftly, Buster put the gun in the hand of the unconscious man. Getting a finger on the trigger, he bent the unresistant arm so that the muzzle of the gun was pointed directly at the head of him who now held it. Carefully squeezing the hand that held the gun, Buster scored a neat hole in the head.

Buster walked away from the two stiffening bodies without a backward glance. The whole episode on the lawn of the peaceful little park had taken less than two minutes. The big black car sped away and into the city.

Not many blocks away, this same night, a bored and lonely-looking man sat drinking at the bar of Joe Cannelli's TROC. The barroom was deserted except for a blonde who was obviously waiting for someone. Obviously anyone.

Conversation between the smirking, willowly, bartender and the lone male customer was desultory.

"I've always heard that Bay City was really gay," the man offered rather pointedly.

As if he'd used a password, which in a sense he had, the bartender became at once effusively chummy.

"Well, my dear, it all depends on what you're looking for."

He leered toward the blonde along the counter with a questioning lift of an eyebrow.

"Oh, heaven no, not that," said the customer.

Both laughed shrilly in their quickly found intimacy.

"But where, I ask you, can one get a man?"

The nymph behind the bar pouted prettily. "Oh, the things you say, Nellie!" Then leaning forward confidentially, he rambled on effusively, illustrating each point with fluttering gestures of his hands and slim hips. "Of course, you can cruise the main drag—that's Market. You might pick up a service man."

At the customer's expression of distaste, the gay bartender went on:

"Yes, they can be rough! So much dirt nowadays. Well, there's the Square. Always a lot of hustlers around there . . . but so shop-worn I always say . . . being pawed over on the bargain counter." He laughed shrilly at his own wit, then continued, "And there's the Baths, too. They're really best in the long run. Costs you a few bucks, my dear. But goodness! There are always two or three dozen there, and you can simply take your pick. It's the best go in Bay City, I'm sure."

"But, aren't they all gay, too? In the baths, I mean? I've never been in one."

"Well, yes," agreed the bartender. "Most that go there are. Of course everyone wanders around stripped,

44

and sometimes you can get so interested in something that you don't stop to consider the breed." Again the shrill, fluttery laugh. "But if you just ask for one of the house masseures when you check in, they see to it that you really get something!"

"I'll bet," dryly commented the customer, finishing his drink. "I don't know if I want a massage."

"Silly boy!" gurgled the man behind the bar. Writing an address on a bit of paper, he passed it over the plank. "Try this place. Just tell them that the bartender at Joe Cannelli's sent you."

Laughing again as the patron turned away eagerly, address clutched in his hand, the gay drink dispenser said gayly, "That one! 'Massage', he says! I don't even think that joint has running water."

CHAPTER SIX

At police headquarters, the following morning, there was unusual activity in and about the homicide squad. A good deal of it centered about the veteran Captain Starr. When his phone announced that Tiger Olsen would like to see him, the Captain briefly said, "Send him up."

A few minutes later Olsen came into the office and greeted the busy detective.

"Hi ya, Tiger," returned Starr. "And what brings you here today of all days? If it's a parking ticket, I'll throw you out bodily."

"Whatsa matter, man?" Tiger teased, "is crime on the increase?"

"Oh brother! And have I got a thing here. A suicide and a murder in the park, and no apparent reason for either one."

"Maybe you'd better hire a detective agency, huh?" laughed Olsen.

Starr bristled momentarily, then asked, "What's that supposed to mean?"

"Well, John, I'm going to work for one of the agencies—sort of a leg man, I guess. But I need a license, or permit, don't I?"

"What agency?" snapped the Captain.

"Morley."

"Oh, no! Tiger, not that character." At this the officer laughed hilariously. "Don't tell me you've become one of the boys?"

"Starr, I think you're wrong about that guy."

"My! It does sound like you two have gotten together at that. You sure surprise me, Tiger. Never thought you'd go that route."

"Look, Starr—" Olsen was obviously annoyed at Starr's implication. He went on: "Yeah, we got together. Down at Sandy's Gym. Morley knocked me on my ass twice in five minutes, just for thinking what you think."

"Oh, no! You mean that guy can fight, too?"

"That I do." Olsen rubbed his jaw reminiscently.

"Well, then, why the hell does he act—"

"I don't know Captain," Olsen cut in. "Maybe it's

some kind of Eastern gag. But he's okay with me, and I'm going to work for him. Now, about that permit, or whatever I'll need . . ."

Shaking his head in bewilderment, Captain Starr said, "Sure, Tiger. You have to furnish a bond with some bonding company."

"Yeah, I've got that. Had to have it when I went to work for Chadwick."

"And," continued the officer, "I suppose that you want to carry a gun, too?"

"I've got a permit and a gun," snapped Olsen.

"What!" gasped the other, "no mascara brush?"

Olsen grinned. "Boy, you're sure in a foul humor today. What's eating you, John?"

"The 'boys' again! I'm gonna suggest to the Commissioner that we have a special department just to handle the gay ones." Starr laughed abruptly. "Maybe your rough, tough Mr. Morley could help us out."

"Okay, okay. Who's done what to whom? Besides, I thought we had a vice squad," said Olsen.

"Oh sure, we've got a vice squad. Under Captain Morphy." Starr's tone was more or less caustic. "Morph's a good policeman. Thirty years on the force. Vice to him consists of three things; gambling, dope, and 'hoors.' He don't like all three, but he understands them. Now, since the war, we've got this new thing in Bay City. Everyone calls them 'gay.' We have gay bars, gay parks, gay clubs, theaters and hotels. In fact, I understand that there are even certain places that these guys can go and get serviced, at a price, with whatever they want."

"You mean . . . houses, like?"

"That's right," continued Starr. "And it's all a matter of opinion whether these guys are criminals or not. We do keep special files on them, and records of their hangouts and so on. But sometimes you just don't know. They turn up in all kinds of places. We find two guys necking in a dark place. One turns out to be a commander in the Navy and the other a prominent attorney."

Oh, no," laughed Olsen. "What did you do with them?"

"What can we do? We've got some younger judges these days, pretty smart guys, too; and tolerance seems to be the word. That pair was vagged, mostly so we could get them on the record. They were given thirty days suspended. After all, they were grown men; there were no minors involved; and what they were doing was probably anti-social, but hardly criminal."

Tiger shook his head. "Well, John, what is there about all this that has you so riled up today?"

The police officer leaned back more comfortably in his chair. "It'll be in all the afternoon papers, so I guess it's no secret. A man walking his dog early this morning found these two in the park—or rather the dog found them. They weren't hidden particularly, just off the sidewalk and near some bushes. One had been shot between the eyes, and the other through the head, as if he had aimed at his mouth. The gun that did both jobs was in this one fellow's hand, and a nitrate test showed it had been in his hand when fired. On the surface, a clear case of murder and suicide."

"No sign of robbery?"

Starr shook his head. "On the contrary; that was the first peculiar angle. One of these guys, a Kay Dunbar, had the other guy's billfold in his hand. It only had a few dollars in it. In his pocket Dunbar had his own wallet with about a hundred bucks in it. Both men had good watches and minor jewelry. The next question was what were they in the park for? The district prowl car went by that place about midnight—had their spotlight on all those bushes and the lawn. They weren't there then, though the doctor says that the shootings were at about that time. Another peculiar feature is that the other one, a guy named Harry Parsons—had the gun in his right hand. His sister says Harry was definitely left-handed. He had polio once, and never completely regained the use of his right hand, though it looked perfectly normal."

"But what makes you think that they were 'that way'?"

"That's the rub. I told you that we have a pretty extensive file on these people. Kay Dunbar has been arrested several times, usually on a lewd-vag charge. Now there's a new development with him; the medics report that he was on dope. There was no narcotics notation previously. He seems to have some money, but he was listed with us as an unemployed entertainer."

"Yeah," grinned Olsen "What did you have on Harry Parsons?"

"Parsons was arrested a year ago for writing a nasty invitation on the walls of the men's room in a park. Arresting officers at the time said that he broke down and admitted perverted practices. However, as he was not actually caught in an act, he was fined a few dollars for defacing city property. He had a very good job as chief accountant for a wholesale garment company. As far as we know yet, his accounts are all in good order."

"Well, captain, what does it all add up to?"

"Too early to tell you yet, but I've got a hunch this was murder both ways. You get sort of a feeling after while."

The men talked a little longer about the license for Olsen and came to a satisfactory arrangement. At the door, the football player turned, with a grin, and said, "I still think you should consult a good detective agency."

"Say!" said Starr, his face unsmiling, "That might be an idea. An agency with a gay detective . . ."

CHAPTER SEVEN

Hattie Campbell felt more confident when she opened the door of the office at nine that morning. For one thing, the line of eager, would-be detectives was not in evidence. For another, there was the comforting thought that Francis had hired a competent assistant.

When he told her of his decision amidst the confusion of the previous afternoon, it had taken her a minute to completely understand the good news. Her initial comment had been, "Oh no, Francis! Not someone who didn't even go through the mill!"

"Oh, but yes, Miss Campbell," Francis had replied.

"Our new man is Mr. Olsen." Francis added with a smug titter, "And from the way you gave him the eye, I suspect that he's quite satisfactory with you, too."

"Bless you, boy. He's the handiest person we've had around this place since your late uncle."

"Well, dearie, don't get a gleam in your eye. I saw him first—or did I? Anyway, he'll move into the small office. Better get someone to put his name on the door. And, I do hope it's all neat and tidy—the office, that is."

Hattie went to her desk and opened the appointment book to familiarize herself with the activities of the new day. When Francis breezed in at ten, she gave him a quick critical inspection. She was pleased to note that his eyes were not lined with red as they had been the previous day.

"Has Tiger shown up yet?" he asked.

Hattie shook her head.

"Send him into my office when he comes in." Francis strode toward the door marked PRIVATE. But he didn't quite get inside his office for at this point the outer door of the reception room opened to admit a haughty, mink-draped lady. She was preceded by a bust like the prow of a battleship. Coming to a stop in the center of the room, she blinked at both Francis and Hattie through raised lorgnettes before inquiring, "And which of you ladies is Morley?"

Hattie giggled aloud as Francis, in sepulchrally formal tones, replied, "I am Mr. Morley, Madame. You, I presume, are Mrs. Bagbones?"

The dowager snorted, then grinned. "Don't be fresh,

young man. I am very nearsighted, and I made an excusable error. Yes, I am Mrs. Bagnold—and you are going to find my Emir."

With a significant glance at Hattie and then at the intercom on her desk, Francis maneuvered the busom lady into his office. After being seated, Mrs. Bagnold peered around through her glass. "Humph! Not what I expected at all, young man. Thought you private eyes always had a bottle on the desk, and a long divan on which to—er—interrogate your female clients."

Francis had decided that this mad old girl had a very subtle sense of humor, and was actually enjoying herself. He played along in an entirely serious manner and answered, "Madame, my secretary, Miss Campbell, whom you saw in the outer office does all of this agency's drinking. My assistant, Mr. Olsen, is definitely the ladies aid. And now, Mrs. Bagnold, just where did you lose—er—the Emir?"

"If I knew that, young man—"

"Of course. Perhaps if we take it easier. The Emir, he is a stranger here in Bay City?"

"Why certainly! My sister sent him on from Rochester. She'd had him for a year, and I suppose that she'd just begun to tire of him. She wrote that he had begun to want so many things, and was even bringing his—er—lady friends home with him. But she fixed that!"

"Well, he certainly sounds like a charming house guest, and not one to get lost, either."

Mrs. Bagnold beamed in agreement. "Now that's

what I would have said, too. We hardly had time to get acquainted."

"How old was His Highness?"

"Oh, quite young, but with such strong haunches. You know—that makes all the difference."

Slightly taken aback by this frankness on the part of his very first client, and quite aware of Hattie giggling in the outer office where she was raptly listening in on this peculiar conversation, Francis hastily agreed. "I'm sure that they do, Madame. Is there a possibility that the Emir has—er—accepted someone else's hospitality? Did he take his things?"

"Ooh, dear no!" said Mrs. Bagnold, "I so wanted him to be happy with me. Then, for company, when I was not handy, there were the three Persian girls. They could certainly have kept him amused, now don't you think, Mr. Morley?"

"The three Persian—?"

"Yes! there are three, mind you. They live with me, too. But I just decided that we could all use a male in the house, and then my sister wrote about the Emir."

"It sounds ideal, I'm sure. Now, did the Emir speak to you before he left?"

"Well, we are more or less strangers yet, though he spent a very restless night in my bedroom."

With some asperity, Francis suggested, "Perhaps, Madame, he didn't care to be locked in anyone's bedroom all night . . ."

Here Francis had the grace to blush. He wondered if all his clients would be so frank.

"Perhaps," admitted Mrs. Bagnold, "but he didn't sleep a wink, just up and down the whole night."

"Well—er—yes, Madame. Perhaps I'd better have a more detailed description. If you can give me the Emir's approximate age, his height, weight, general features—"

"Frankly, Mr. Morley, I've been so busy, what with one thing and another, I really never took a very good look at him. I'm so near-sighted.

Francis looked up suddenly from the scanty notes that he had made. Out of nowhere an utterly impossible thought had popped into his mind—impossible, of course. "Pardon me, Mrs. Bagnold, did you say the Emir was from Afghanistan?"

"Why of course! He's actually Siamese. That's only his real registration name—'Emir of Afghanistan.'"

Simultaneously with muted convulsive strangling noises over the intercom, it all became quite clear to Francis. As if to reassure himself, however, he asked in a menacing monotone—"Mrs. Bagnold, are we discussing a cat?"

"But certainly, young man."

"And I understand that he's a young Siamese, with husky haunches?"

"Blue eyes," added Mrs. Bagnold.

"Blue eyes, just here from Rochester; and you have never really taken a good look at him?"

"Why, yes. That's—"

Francis rose and went to the door, which he opened unsmilingly. "Mrs. Bagnold, the Morley Agency always gets its man! It is now just after ten. We will have the Emir at your home before five o'clock."

The lady also moved to the door, sensing, perhaps, the slight pique in which Francis found himself.

"That, young man, will surely be service."

"And may I suggest, Madame, that you leave your address at the desk, and, er, your check, if you please," Francis added as he courteously bowed the lady out and closed the door with a sigh of relief.

In a few minutes, Hattie entered following a perfunctory knock.

"Francis, I've got all of it on tape! If you ever feel dull or blue, I'll give you a playback."

She was highly amused at the pained expression on Francis' face.

". . . and he was up and down all night," she murmured.

"Please, Minnie, I'm thinking."

"You'd better be thinking where the Emir might be."

"Oh, poo on the Emir. After a night locked in that old bat's boudoir, I doubt if he'll ever come back."

"Francis! you promised—and before five o'clock. And we do have her check for two hundred and fifty dollars."

"That's the point, dearie. Okay, here's what you do. Call some pet shops. You want a young Siamese, with strong haunches, brown ears, blue eyes—"

"Yes, Mr. Morley. I've got all that. And, y'know, most Siamese do look alike. They are either brown points or blue. But—"

57

"The old girl is blind anyway, and she said that she had hardly taken a good look at him. Besides he was a stranger there, too; so I think that this will work. Get the beast sent up here. When Tiger comes in, I'll have him take it out."

"Okay, boss, if you say so," Hattie seemed a little dubious.

"I do say so. And, Hattie, this will show a neat profit for the agency. Besides," Francis laughed lightly, "according to all the stories circulating, what private eye is ethical, anyhow?"

Tiger walked in full of news about the events at the police station, but soon he found himself headed for the Bagnold residence, gingerly bearing a neat wicker traveling cage, with one Siamese meowing loudly within.

A very brief inspection had confirmed brown ears, blue eyes, and redoubtable haunches. The bored feline seemed to think fully as little of his viewers as they did of him. Much to Francis' surprise, even this unregistered specimen was worth $75.00, at least to the dealer who had sent him. However, being in no mood for a further discussion of cats, Francis had merely waved a glass casually over the lip-lifting pussy, and said, "Butch, I now christen thee the 'Emir of Afghanistan, the Second,' and I advise you to watch the old gal after midnight."

Tiger had hardly gone on his way with the restive beast, when the phone rang. The connection switched to Francis, and he answered tiredly. To his complete surprise, it was Captain Starr of the Bay City Homicide Dept.

"Morley? I'm sending a young lady over to see you."

"Well, that's nice. Whatever for?"

Francis was amused at the slightly belligerent tone of the officer when he said,

"Now look, Morley, this office has a policy of always working with you private investigators, when and where possible. You people can often do favors for us, and in return we can often help you. Now this young lady is searching for her brother, who has been missing a week—"

"But, Captain Starr," Francis interrupted, "the agency, that is, Olsen and myself, we want to cooperate fully with the police. But I just don't see . . ."

"All right, all right! Let me tell it. Did Olsen tell you anything about a case that we discussed over here?"

"Oh, Captain, we're saving all that chit-chat for bedtime."

"Now look here, Morley!" angrily exclaimed the officer.

Francis giggled, and then, more seriously, apologized for his joking. He continued, "Yes, Captain, he just had time to mention something about those two guys in the park."

"Okay, then, er, did Olsen tell you that our records showed—that is, er, what kind of fellows they were?"

"But, of course, Captain Starr! What other kind of men would be found in each other's arms in a public park, even dead?"

"Please, Morley, I'm trying to be serious." the officer added reluctantly, "I think that we could use your help in this."

Francis recognized a quality in Starr's voice that would brook very little more foolishness. He decided to be serious.

"All right, Captain Starr. I will try not to imagine that there is anything personal about all this. You have two characters, shot in a park. Your records show that both were practicing homos—right?"

"Yes. Now that's . . ." the detective hesitated.

"Probably what you are trying to say, in your own coy way—and strictly impersonally, of course—is that you suspect that I, too, am a nervous type. Okay, think what you like, Captain," snapped Francis. "Now having cleared that much away, how can the Morley Agency assist the Police Department? And what has this woman's missing brother got to do with it?"

"That's what I'm trying to explain to you. You see, this, er, personality angle is way beyond my bunch over here. I don't have a man available who could possibly understand these people. I feel, that, shall I say, that perhaps you do, er . . ."

"Yes, Captain Starr. Get on with it," Francis said grimly.

"So, here's the connection. If you came into this case as a private investigator, with a client, that is, and looking for the girl's missing brother, then maybe we could work together on it. I've got a hunch that this is all part of something big—like I told Tiger."

"But, Captain, I'm still not sure that I get the connection. This girl . . ."

"Oh, you didn't let me finish. You see, I know where Vivien Holden's brother is . . ."

"You what! Then why—?"

"Now, wait a minute. He's been in the morgue since last night, though I haven't told her so. The body was found in the surf, out at the beach. The face had been pretty badly beaten up, and there were some other funny details. I'll tell you more about that later. The point is, I want you to get all this before she arrives at your office. Aside from this other stuff, Art Holden had been shot by the same gun that killed those two fairi—pardon! those two guys in the park!"

CHAPTER EIGHT

Though very little more of Starr's call had made any sensible pattern, Francis had finally registered the idea that the detective captain believed that there was a series of murders, all somehow connected with crime based on vice in Bay City. The officer had insinuated that perhaps a partial investigation of this murder-vice ring by the Agency could be more revealing than if conducted along the lines of official police procedure.

Francis admired the police officer's grasp of the situation, as well as his ability to visualize the most unorthodox use of the Agency. And, as he thought out the possible personal involvement in the matter, he mused, "This is certainly no Emir to contend with . . . !"

Half an hour later Hattie ushered a slight brunette, dressed in a becoming suit and a smart fur piece, into his office. Francis, rising, smilingly indicated the comfortable chair before the desk, negligently flipping the intercom key to 'open.' He then walked to the window and adjusted the venetian blinds slowly and carefully in order to give his secretary a chance to get ready to record whatever might be forthcoming. During this time he chatted lightly while covertly inspecting the client who sat tensely in the chair.

"Miss Holden . . . I'm sure that Captain Starr said it was 'Miss'?" The girl merely nodded in reply.

As she seemed at a troubled loss as to what to say, Francis said, "I believe that Captain Starr said you were looking for your brother?" At the girl's nodded affirmation, he continued, "Well now, Miss Holden, it's not quite clear to me—why should the Homicide Department be interested in a Missing Person? There is, as I presume you know, a very efficient and complete department—"

Here he was interrupted by a rapid and evidently pent-up outburst from the pretty, dark-haired young woman.

"Mr. Morley, I've been just frantic—just crazy with anxiety since Arthur's disappearance—"

Francis deliberately raised a hand to interrupt. While her speech was swift and seemed to tumble out, it was obviously the talk and manner of a person of culture and refinement.

"Miss Holden, please, pardon me for just one moment, and let's take this easily . . ." He doubted, by the way her tiny, even teeth caught at her full red lip, that the girl would be able to discuss her affairs sensibly and quietly, but he hoped for coherence at any rate. "Just when did your brother—Arthur Holden, is it?—when did he disappear?"

"But that's the point, Mr. Morley," she replied with noticeable restraint. "It was almost a week ago. Arthur has been nervous and worried for several days. Then the bank had called about the overdraft—"

Francis again interrupted, partially to calm the overwrought young woman.

"I see. Now what exactly was it about the bank? I mean to say, aside from his nervousness, was this call the first indication that something was wrong?"

"Yes, yes!" she replied, and went on, "you see, we have several accounts. One is the estate's—we are orphans—"the client briefly interpolated. "And then there is a service account for actual expenses, and a general checking fund on which either of us may draw. But whenever we do draw on this account, we always tell each other; then, if it happens to be at a time before any regular dividend is due from the investments, we jointly transfer covering funds from the estate account to the general checking account." Here the young lady smiled fleetingly. Perhaps she had recognized Francis' delaying tactic for its kindly motive. In any case, she continued quite calmly, "I know all this is confusing, but it's really a part of it, to me; because it is all a reason why Arthur shouldn't have gone away. You see, the bank called that he had cashed a check for more than was actually in the account, and of course I told them at once that our jointly signed estate check would be promptly forthcoming."

Francis nodded in understanding, though he as yet failed to see where all this was leading. His smile, however again elicited a like and charming demonstration from the client as she continued:

"I spoke to Arthur that very evening and suggested we go to the bank together in the morning. I did not ask why he had drawn out such a large amount. I think it was thirty-seven hundred. Mr. Morley, please understand that he has a perfect right to the money if he wishes. But anyway, he was moody and upset the whole evening, saying only that he would take care of it in the morning. Then he went to his room. I just happened to answer when the phone rang some time later. This person demanded very rudely to speak to my brother. I thought perhaps that Arthur had gone to bed and I wouldn't like to disturb him, so I asked who was calling. Well, this man, or woman, was very insistent that I tell Arthur that it was a Kay Dunbar calling. Of course, I went up to call him.

For the first time, Francis nodded with some understanding. The girl continued:

"He seemed very excited when I spoke to him, and went to the phone at once. I remained upstairs, and so I heard none of their short conversation. But it was only a minute before Arthur came quickly up the stairs.

"I tried to stop him for a minute, asking if I could

be of any help, but he only said roughly that he had to go out. I assumed he was going to meet this Dunbar person. A few minutes later, Arthur left our apartment."

Here her braveness momentarily deserted her, and tears glistened in her attractive eyes.

"That was the last time in almost a week that I have seen him. I've been waiting for some word from him, every minute of the day and night. I've checked all the hospitals and contacted all our friends, and I've kept reading almost every new edition of the papers as they came out—" Here her rushing words came to an abrupt halt, and once again she was tensed and excited. "So," she continued, "this afternoon when the papers came and I read the little bit there was about those two men found in that park, and—well, there was that name, Kay Dunbar . . ."

Francis courteously handed her his handkerchief. The girl was really crying now. He made some solicitous and conventional remarks, adding, "And so now I see. That's why you went to the Homicide office?"

"Yes," the brunette nodded affirmation. "And the first man that I talked to was horrid. He seemed to think that I was enquiring about Dunbar, and he said some things about him that were absolutely bestial . . ."

Again Francis tried to soothe the distraught girl, and was partially successful. "I know, Miss Holden. Some of these cops are pretty rough. Of course, if your brother knew this man . . ."

His statement really demanded an answer, and after

66

a pause, during which she wiped away her tears, the client nodded.

Very primly, she said, "Yes, Mr. Morley, I do know about such things. I studied social services in college, I became reconciled some years back to the fact that my brother has little interest in women, as such . . ." This she said bravely and unflinchingly. But as if in justification, she added, "He isn't however, the extreme type. There isn't anything particularly noticeable, or 'gay'—I think that's the common expression now—about Arthur. But all that could hardly be the reason for him to go away like this."

"Is there any possibility that your brother is, or was, being blackmailed by this Dunbar?"

The Holden girl brightened at this suggestion, but in a moment, as if she'd had the same consecutive idea that Francis had had, she was again obviously upset.

"That's what I thought, too. But—but then these men were both shot, and with a small automatic. And now Arthur has disappeared." Again the girl seemed near to hysteria.

Francis came around the desk and patted her heaving shoulders. In an effort to ease her tenseness, he softly promised, "Come now, Miss Holden, we'll find Arthur for you." He felt like a Judas as he did so.

At his, the girl's sobbing stopped. She raised appealing tear-drenched eyes to the attractive young man at her side.

"Oh, thank you. But there is something else. Can

I, dare I, be completely frank with you, Mr. Morley?"

Francis smiled receptively. "I hope you have been, Miss Holden."

"Yes, it's all true, what I've told you. But there is more. And I'm so mixed up, I just don't know who to trust."

"Please, Miss Holden. Whatever you tell me here cannot go any further, particularly, if we are to locate your brother. The Agency should have every possible detail. Then, with the full cooperation of the police—"

At this last word, the girl again cried out, "Oh, no! Mr. Morley, I didn't tell Captain Starr quite everything."

"No, Miss Holden? Perhaps you'd better—"

"Will he have to be told everything I tell you, every detail? she asked anxiously.

"Well . . ." Under the very peculiar circumstances, Francis hesitated. But with the mental reassurance that this whole conversation was being recorded, he continued, "Ordinarily, any information that an agency has from a client is 'privileged,' if you understand. . . ."

"Yes, yes, I know," the girl hastily agreed.

"Except in a case of murder," Francis added.

At his last, the brunette blanched, revealing at least that her former remarkable coloring was natural.

Francis continued, "As there is no connection here between your brother's knowing Dunbar, and Dunbar's murder, I believe that I can safely say that Arthur Holden will, in consequence, suffer no further embarrassment."

Francis felt like a fraud and a cheat as he made this

true if ambiguous statement, knowing as he did that Holden—in the morgue—was indeed safely beyond any embarrassment.

The sister, however, was content to grasp at the hope of his words. In a more relieved tone, she said, "Oh, that's different, though I just don't see how it all fits in. You see, while I was talking with Captain Starr, someone brought in a small tagged automatic and gave it to him. The Captain must have noticed me looking at it, for he briefly explained that it was the weapon used to kill Dunbar and that other person—" Here she hesitated again, as if still undecided.

"Yes?—and?" prompted Francis.

"That's what I didn't tell the police. That was Arthur's gun."

The girl had hardly finished with this revealing statement when Hattie interrupted to tell Francis that Mr. Olsen had returned. Asking that his assistant be instructed to join him, Francis explained to his client that the Agency staff would start at once on an extensive search for her brother.

At this point, Tiger came into the private office. After introductions had been made, Francis suggested that he see Miss Holden to her apartment, and perhaps get some further details about the missing man. He assured the young woman as she was leaving that he had complete confidence in his assistant's discretion, and suggested that she could feel free to tell Olsen anything that might help in locating her brother. Francis purposely did not give

Tiger his own information of the brother's whereabouts, feeling that without the knowledge Olsen might glean even more pertinent information.

This Tiger seemed to be well on the way of doing as he left with his charge. Smiling infectiously and with suitable light conversation, he was already charming the petite brunette as they turned to leave the Agency. However, just as Tiger and the pretty client were at the door, the brunette turned suddenly to Francis.

"Mr. Morley! I just remembered. The diary." Arthur has kept a diary for years. At least he used to. When we were smaller he sometimes read it to me." She sighed, at the memory. "It's been some years since I've actually seen it, or since he has mentioned it, but I do think that he still keeps it. Perhaps if I can locate it among his things—"

"That would be fine," Francis said enthusiastically. "If you do find it, please bring it right in," he urged.

As the outer office door closed finally on the pair, Francis dropped onto a divan in the reception room. "My beads, dearie! What a day! Did you get all that in there, Hattie?"

"Certainly. It's on tape for posterity," said the secretary.

"Well, Minnie, I'm going out for awhile. I'd hate to get in the habit of keeping regular hours. What would the boys think! Transfer all calls to the phone service when you leave. I'll call 'em later and let 'em know where I am. And you, you go straight home, dearie. Never mind those big marines on the streets," he added lightly.

"Yeah? Well that goes for you, too." gayly replied the secretary, though she blushed furiously as she said it.

"Well!" Francis softly exclaimed to himself. "First the Tiger, then that one. Could be my slip is showing . . ." He grinned roguishly as he reached for the door.

CHAPTER NINE

Captain Starr stolidly eyed the group of men gathered in his office. Despite the late hour their conversation, with many interruptions and developments, had already lasted over three hours. Nevertheless those present appeared to be alertly interested in the summary the Homicide officer now offered. The only dissenting note came as an occasional scowl from the greying, paunchy man who sat beside Starr behind the desk. This man had been introduced to Francis as Captain Morphy, the head of the Bay City Vice Squad.

Even at the outset, Captain Morphy had been openly

and scornfully hostile. Mouthing a large cigar, he had barely repeated Francis' name upon Starr's introduction. He was at once slightly dazed as Francis gushingly remarked, while giving a flashing display of limp-wristed gesture:

"Oh, Captain Morphy! And of the Vice Squad! Well! I've certainly wanted to meet you."

"Yeah?" Morphy, cigar clutched in a ham-like fist in mid-air, stood open mouthed.

"Dear me, yes!" Francis giggled coyly. "It seems we have so many friends in common."

Morphy turned threateningly to Captain Starr. "What the hell is this, a gag?"

Even the taciturn Starr was amused, but he placatingly nudged the vice officer into a seat next to his own. His glare at Francis had a twinkle, as he brusquely said, "Okay, Morph, you're being kidded. And you too, Morley—knock it off."

The men present then discussed the situation for some time, until the phone announced another visitor. This man proved to be the lonesome one who'd been guided on his way by the bartender at Joe Cannelli's TROC bar. He was evidently known to the officers, who greeted him with respect. Captain Starr explained to Francis that this gentleman, representing 'another government agency,' was interested in the narcotic traffic. That there now seemed to be some tie-in between these three murders and the dope traffic. Captain Starr now offered his summary of the matter.

"All right, then. Now as far as we know at this

73

time, we have that gun, and we know that the first to die, Holden, was its owner.

There appears to be some evidence that Holden was being blackmailed. He got together nearly four thousand dollars, and, at a call from Dunbar, went to meet him. He next appears washed up on the beach—without the money. He had been very badly beaten about the face, but he had been killed with a bullet from the gun."

Here Francis interrupted, "Which came first?—the beating or the bullet?"

Both the police captains glared at Morley, but Starr patiently answered the question.

"The morgue lab seems to think that he was shot first, then beaten afterwards. Maybe the idea was to destroy his identity."

"Okay," Francis said, "I only asked."

"Sure, sure."

"Now here is where it may all be guess work. It is the expressed opinion of Holden's sister that her brother was 'one of the boys.'" The Homicide officer glared around to assure himself that he was understood. "And as there is no other apparent connection, it is possible that he was being blackmailed because of some such activity. Now this is partially confirmed by the fact that his last known contact seems to have been Dunbar, who had a long record of active if petty homosexuality. Also, Dunbar must have been in some racket that paid off, because he didn't work and always had plenty of spending money. But—and in this connection—Dunbar had also become a narcotics user during the past year.

"Now, when these two subsequent, er, men were found murdered—and we are quite sure that both Dunbar and Parsons were murdered by the same gun that had killed Holden—we put the usual pick-up order on all known associates and similar vice characters. This was with the help of Captain Morphy . . . ," this last with a placating glance at the still disgruntled vice-squad leader, ". . . and, while we have nothing as yet that seems pertinent to these three killings, we do find that of the 'gay' boys arrested, there are now over twice as many heroin users as there were in a similar pickup a year ago. This, I believe, is also checked out by another set of records."

The narcotics agent nodded in agreement and Starr continued,

"And so it begins to look as though we have several connected problems on our hands. First, we have three known killings. Then, we may have an organized blackmail racket. And now, we have a narcotics distribution. All three seem to be tied in with the people in this 'gay' group."

Here the federal man put in a word.

"Believe me, gentlemen, from the size of this distribution, as far as the narcotics are concerned, this is big business. One thing puzzles me, though, Captain Morphy. Why does Bay City have such an overlarge percentage of these queer people? They seem to be actually encouraged here. Why, they even have their own clubs and bars. I may be old-fashioned, but I just don't get this local tolerance."

Francis sniffed audibly, then said,

"I seem to recall that several hundred federal government employees have been loudly bounced in Washington lately, and for just such little peccadillos . . ."

Morphy, the vice-squad officer, shook his head wearily.

"Yeah. And sometimes I don't get it either. Y'see, this town used to be wide open. It was the talk of the world, being a seaport and all. Things were pretty much under control, and everyone was making a little money. Then these people that always want to clean up everything lost out on prohibition, so they decided to run all the 'hoors' out of town. Finally, we had to close up all those quiet, friendly, well-regulated houses . . ." The officer sighed reminiscently.

"Sounds cozy," murmured Francis.

The policeman ignored this, and continued: "Now, this is a sailor's town. It was once a great port. I guess these young fellas today just gotta do something with the time on their hands."

As the vice officer paused, the federal man asked, "But why all these open fag bars and joints?"

"Oh, that's pretty simple to explain, I guess. Personally, I always want to plant a foot in those cuties' butts, but the new Commission has psychiatrists who advise that these people should be allowed to congregate in their own places. I suppose that it does eliminate a lot of possible friction—fights and stuff that might get started in regular joints. For their own protection, too.

The government agent shook his head, "It still

76

doesn't make sense to me, even though these people aren't actually criminals."

Francis snickered audibly at this.

Captain Starr hastily brought the discussion to order with a terse, "It certainly looks like this gang we're dealing with are criminals; and we've got to get to them fast. Now, gentlemen, this is my idea; Mr. Morley here is practically a stranger in the city. Moreover, he is a licensed operator of a private agency. He, er, that is, well, ahem, he wants to cooperate with the department. And as he has every appearance . . ." Starr bogged down for a moment, actually blushing, and distinctly at a loss for words.

Francis, for the first time during the conference, abandoned his flippant attitude and took up where the captain had paused.

"Gentlemen, let's face it. Suppose we put it this way, and stop mincing words . . ." Strangely, his words were now clipped and sincere; his tone was distinguished by a dangerous steely quality, ". . . our immediate target seems to be a gang, or organization, that blackmails and dopes the 'boys.' "

Turning to the government agent, Francis continued, "I understand from what you said before that you tried to work your way into a few places, but you just didn't seem to fit. The point seems to be that I look more the type, and can probably crash this outfit somewhere. I'm willing to try to find out where the racket centers and where the stuff is pushed. As I see it, there must be some central spot. And the question is—where is it?" Francis looked around at the three officers questioningly, but received no answer or comment. "All right now here is a thought that came to me when Captain Starr told us about Holden. If he was shot first and beaten later, this all must have taken some time. Were his clothes bloodied, Captain Starr?"

The homicide officer shook his head. "I'd say no to that. The body had been in the surf for some time, but as I recall there were no bloodstains on the collar of his white shirt."

Maybe he had his shirt off," mused Francis.

"Where was Holden killed? That might be our spot. Now I suggest that we all go down and take another look at the late Mr. Holden and his things. Maybe one of us will get a new idea. What do you say, Captain Starr?"

The big officer nodded his approval. "It's a good place to start. Follow me."

A few minutes later the men were in the cellar of the police station. Spread out on the work table before them were all the personal effects of the late Arthur Holden, whose body they had just examined. The suit of clothes, though soiled and salt-stiffened from its time in the ocean, was of obvious quality. Francis mentally catalogued the usual men's attire.

"Is this everything?" he asked.

"The works," glibly answered the attendant.

Francis insisted: "No wallet, papers, jewelry—anything like that?"

78

The morgue man only shrugged, and indicated the coarse manila envelope whose contents—a case of keys, a single long flat key on a rubber band, a pair of cuff links, and a tie-clasp—were spread out on the table.

"Do you remember what pockets these were in?" asked Francis.

"Why, yes. It happens that I received him and I do." The attendant hesitated, then explained, "Y'see, we usually go through all the pockets and check for jewelry the first thing."

Captain Morphy snorted. "Yeah! I'll bet."

The other grinned, and, a little vehemently, the morgue man insisted, "Think what you like, but this is all that was on him. Say, I remember something funny, though. This key on the rubber band, it was shoved way up on his arm, up past his elbow."

Examining the key more closely, the narcotics man suddenly exclaimed: "Say! I've seen this before, or rather, one just like it. You remember I told you that I went to the baths? Well, they give you a key like this for the small room that you get. It's got a bed and a chair and some hangers for clothes. You're supposed to put the towel they give you around yourself and then you wander around." He paused, momentarily flushing at the recollections that came to him.

Francis broke the brief silence by exclaiming excitedly: "That's it, then!"

"That's what?" demanded Captain Starr.

"That must have been where he was killed. Look, Captain, don't you see what is missing here?"

Both of the detective officers again looked over the scattered garments. Then Starr answered, "Why, sure. His watch, billfold—"

"No, Captain. No!" Francis interrupted. "I mean his underwear. Shorts, maybe . . . and a T Shirt, or something. Where are they?"

Involuntarily they all turned to the morgue worker. Sensing their question, he shook his head.

"Uh'uh. He didn't have any on. Just what you see there."

"Well, then, can't you see it!" exclaimed Francis. "He was stripped when they shot him, with just that key on his arm. When they dressed the body to take him out, they just put on the outer clothing, not bothering with the skivies, or the necktie. Look, no tie there," Francis indicated the table. "But there's a tie-clasp. Don't you all see it?"

The homicide chief nodded, though hesitantly, and turned abruptly to the federal man.

"Where is that joint? We'll take it apart!"

Again, Francis interrupted:

"No, Captain. Not that way. I've got a better idea. Suppose I get a party together and take them all to the baths after the bars close. That way Olsen and I can look the place over thoroughly. You can always shake it down afterwards."

Francis grinned as he turned to Captain Morphy and asked, "Where would one of the boys from out of town go to meet some local characters? I mean a nice place, 'gay' but refined . . . expensive?"

80

Unhesitatingly Morphy replied, "The fairies with dough seem to hang out at the Bait Room. That's a joint over on Broadway. They got a bunch of the boys in the floor show, all dressed up like women . . ."

Francis laughed, and even the other two men smiled at the vice officer's expression as Morley, looking completely innocent, asked,

"Honestly! Do they, Captain Morphy? And which one of the chorus is your favorite?"

The stolid officer pondered this a moment before replying. "There's one there, calls himself the King of the Queens. Now he really is pretty—" the Captain broke off with an angry string of obsolete curse words at the amusement he saw on the other faces. When he had exhausted this vocabulary, he added belligerently, "Well, you asked me . . ."

"Okay, so I did," smiled Francis. "Now, let me get at a phone."

As he searched through a small memo book for Vivien Holden's number, Francis added rather cryptically,

"I'll just take along my own rough trade, though, instead of trying the house product . . ."

CHAPTER TEN

High on a hilltop overlooking the city lights, twin-kling in a many-colored magic carpet beneath them, Vivien Holden and Tiger Olsen huddled closer in the sleek little sports roadster. During the several hours since they had left the Agency offices, the couple had become happily and closely acquainted. What had started as simply a tactic to take the beautiful girl's mind off the problem of her missing brother had swiftly flowered into a more personal thing between the two of them. They had had a leisurely dinner in a quiet out-of-the-way spot, during which the attractive young woman had retold

82

much of the information she had already given to Francis Morley. This time, however, with her listener holding her hands in his own, her narrative had been without tears. She felt, somehow, that this brutishly big man who listened so quietly and attentively to her hesitant fears about her brother, his character and his peculiarities, was a protection—a sort of buffer between those strange values and the more usual feeling between a man and a woman. She had welcomed his increasing personal interest and contact.

Suddenly it seemed to come to both of them, seated above the brightly illuminated city, that here was a peace of mind and mutual regard that demanded an even closer, more intimate, expression. The brawny arm about Vivien's shoulders now pulled her roughly but tenderly to a welcomed masculine embrace. As their lips met, seeking and tentative, Tiger could feel the thump of his heart beating against the firm, out-thrust breasts of the girl in his arms. As her feverish lips worked on his own, and her questing tongue sought a reply against his teeth, the big man felt a surge of desire pass through his trembling body.

Her busy tongue found his. His big hands tenderly encircled her ripe resilient breasts. Here, too, he thought in a flash, was a hot body yearning for satisfaction, a pebble-hard erectness that matched the expanding warmth within his own loins. At once Tiger knew that all the many and varied experiences of his life had been merely training for what this night might bring. With a soft reluctance he pulled his lips from her demanding mouth, and tenderly kissing her passion-blurred eyes, murmured, "Oh, God!" Vivien, darling . . . we must!"

With a complete understanding of his throbbing male need, she swayed away from his embrace and, bringing her own taut emotions under control, replied pantingly, "Yes, Tiger. Yes! Tonight—now! My place isn't far."

With a hasty kiss on the tip of her pert nose, Tiger started the car.

Fifteen minutes later, Tiger stared down at the luscious body sprawled on the bed. His eyes swept avidly across the peaks of her hot-tipped breasts, glanced downward to the flattened plain beneath, noted the seductive curve of her hips and the satin skin of her cleanly rounded thighs.

Vivien held her arms out to him. Her own eyes candidly inspected the hardened masculinity of him as he responded immediately to her wanton invitation.

His hands bruised the rubbery mountains of her breasts, moving with an expert circular motion, forcing the skin to flush from the extent of her aroused desire. Her own hands captured his, held them tightly, then spurred him on to new, more exciting conquests. Her mouth opened, slack with desire. Her eyes misted as she felt his mouth and his hands burn into her flesh, exciting every taut nerve end, probing with exquisite sensation the forbidden treasures of her wildly responding body.

She began to writhe crazily beneath him, churning about on the sheets, frantically grappling to bring him to her, to hold him close in the deep, moist weld of desperate passion.

"Now Tiger," she growled. "Oh Tiger, don't make me wait!"

His entire body became rigid; the massive muscles rippling beneath the skin of his stallion body demanded that he possess her completely, probe the depths of her fantastic passion, feel her answering thrust, goad her to new and higher peaks of excrutiating sensation. He felt her hands on his skin. A shudder of ecstacy went through him. Slowly; he let her have her way. Inch by inch he lowered himself to her, then rested, allowing the magnetic force of desire to grow between them until every nerve was shrieking for fulfillment. Only then did he begin the slow rhythm of love. She moved upon him in a frenzy, but his muscled chest lowered until the white-hot spires of her breasts burned into his flesh. He forced her back into the mattress, forced her to match his own exploratory pace. Only when he was sure that she had relinquished all control to him, did he give his passion full reign.

Then her voice was loud with the power of his love-making, crying out senselessly, aware only of the unbearable sweetness of his attack, the ramrod hardness of his body crushing into the yielding softness of her own answering flesh. Her hands flailed the air, then settled on his back, urging him to her, striating his back with cat-like nails as she engraved the red marks of passion upon his skin.

85

Tiger emitted a roar, a bellow of triumph as her legs wound around his, as her body was caught in a series of spasmodic convulsions that drew the tension from him in a wave of pulsating joy.

Almost two hours later, the dream-like quality of their ecstasy was shattered by the insistent ringing of the telephone. Clasping the woman tightly in his insatiable embrace, Tiger whispered in Vivien's ear, "Darling, let it ring . . . let it ring . . ."

But after another long and passionate moment surrendered to his demands, she pulled away from his arms.

"No, Tiger . . . No! Wait, oh, dearest, please wait. I must answer. It might be Arthur . . ."

He released her reluctantly, as common sense intruded into the magic whirlpool of their coupling. He grunted wryly and snorted, "Huh! Probably a wrong number . . ."

The girl, switched on a soft bedside lamp, and searched about the foot of the disturbed bed for the dressing gown that had been summarily removed from her.

As she rose to put it on, Tiger was again amazed with the tiny, almost fragile appearance of the perfect body, a body whose strength he now knew could equal his own in its demands. Watching her as she left the dainty, feminine bedroom, he sighed with satisfaction at the memory of what they had so recently had for each other. He closed his eyes and slid down into the bed, enjoying in anticipation the further pleasures to come.

Vivien's voice brought him rudely to his senses. Again she stood in the doorway, fists planted comically on her hips, laughing unreservedly. Her unfastened robe hung negligently open, renewing Tiger's pleasure.

"It's for you, you big lug. I think it's your boss."

With a long sigh, Tiger climbed out of the bed and started toward her, unaware and unashamed of his rugged nakedness. Encircling her with his arms, he lifted her up so that their lips were joined in a kiss. He held her, feet off the floor, with all of her lithe body molded to his own. After a moment she pulled her head away, laughing.

"The telephone, stupid. This can wait. . . ."

"Oh, no it can't," he murmured as he nuzzled hungrily at her throat.

Still holding her firmly against himself, he lowered her slowly and gently, their warm sweating bodies sliding easily against each other. For a moment, Vivien, too, was almost carried away by his urgency. But as her toes neared the floor she managed to pull herself away from his stiffening desire.

"Hey, you've got to answer the phone. It's Mr. Morley . . ."

Releasing her, Tiger resignedly turned down the hallway to the telephone. Behind him, with a promising laugh, Vivien happily flopped back on the bed.

Picking up the instrument, Tiger suppressed a yawn, "Yes, boss?"

"Well! Did I disturb something?" Francis chuckled.

"Huh! We were just discussing Arthur," replied Tiger sardonically.

"Oh yeah? Well, never mind that now. Did you find the diary?"

"Uh, well, y'see, boss, we just about got here, and . . ."

"Yes, dear. Mother knows! Now listen, get your clothes on . . ."

Tiger flushed. For the first time, he was aware of his complete nudity. He laughed shakily as Francis continued:

"You and I are going night clubbing."

"Oh, Frank! Tonight?"

"Yes, lover man, tonight! We're going to look for a party."

"Boss," Tiger said confidentially, "I've got a party—"

Francis broke in, "Tiger, this is serious. We've got to find some people, and we can't waste any time at it. So, come on. I'll meet you outside the Bait Room."

"Oh, now boss! Please! That's one of those swish joints."

"You'll be safe, dearie. I'll protect you. And besides, I doubt if any of them could do much good with you tonight . . ."

Tiger laughed. "Boss, you were never more right. Okay, give me half an hour."

Quickly replacing the phone, he strode back toward the bedroom mentally calculating. Fifteen minutes to dress and get there. That gives me fifteen more minutes here. . . .

Actually, Tiger was fifteen minutes late.

CHAPTER ELEVEN

Francis and Tiger met as planned, in the convenient parking lot adjoining the brightly lighted exterior of the Bait Room.

Francis, who had come by cab, paced restlessly up and down as he waited. He had a partially formed plan in his mind by the time Tiger pulled up in his Jaguar. A good deal of Francis' light and disdainful manner had obviously been discarded as he greeted his assistant.

"You're late, Olsen," he snapped, and then removed the sting with, "Probably held up in a good cause, though. Park over there in the corner and let's talk a minute . . ."

After they were comfortably seated in the parked sport car and Olsen had briefly reported that Vivien Holden was safely at home, Francis inquired, "Did she find that diary?"

Tiger flushed. "Well, as a matter of fact, we never did get to look for it. Y'see, after we'd had dinner—"

"Tiger, please, listen to me," interrupted Morley in tones more somber than any Olsen had heard from him previously. "This is serious, to all concerned. To me, to you, the Agency, the police and even to Vivien Holden. You see, Arthur Holden was murdered. I've just come from the Morgue, where I saw his body. Now, here's the story, or part of it. There have been three murders that the police know of, a lot of blackmailing and a busy narcotics ring. And there's almost nothing to go on. Now, because of the peculiar set-up, the police—your Captain Starr, at any rate—think that the Agency can help them in this. I might add that Federal authorities are already mixed up in this as well. Do you begin to get the picture?"

"Wow!" breathed Tiger, "Sounds big. But where do we come in?"

"Well, one of the few things that we do have to go on is the fact that all these people are 'gay' . . . homosexuals."

"Yeah, I follow you."

"There must be some contact in one of these joints they hang out in, like maybe the Bait Room here. Now, another thing. Holden was possibly killed in a gymnasium or in a bath house—or in one of those so-called Turkish Baths. I'll tell you more about that later on. There are

90

a couple of other leads that point the same way. There are five of these 'baths' in the city. One is entirely respectable; one is questionable; and the other three are definitely 'gay' houses."

"Okay, boss. So let's go take a bath."

"It's not as easy as that, Tiger. I am hardly known here, but you are. Now, I figure that if we make some of these joints tonight and pick up a small crowd as we go along, we can all end up in one or more of these baths by morning. That way, it will seem very natural."

Tiger interrupted. "Look, Frank, and don't misunderstand me, but don't you think that I might look a little out of place?"

"Uh-uh! That's the idea. I'm supposed to be a wealthy young thing from the East who has picked you up. This way you can be partially sure of not being bothered by any of those guys. And besides," he added with his former twinkle, "I'm sure that you'll attract a crowd."

After a long and caustic look at his employer, Olsen said, "The crowd had better not crowd me."

"I know, Tiger. But look, no rough stuff if you can help it. These people tell everything to each other, and the word would get around too soon if you got too rough. Please, take it easy, okay?"

After a little more conversation, the two men went into the Bait Room.

This was actually a long barn of a hall, exotically hung with draperies. It was dimly lighted except for the stage at one end and the bar at the other. The space in between was crowded with many small tables which seemed to be all filled. Among the guests were very few women. Most of these were either more masculine in appearance than many of the men about them, or they were part of the several large parties of obvious sight-seers.

On the stage, a man dressed as a woman in a costume that displayed oversized and obviously false breasts sang a song about 'MY MILITARY MAN . . . HE MARCHES ON MY FRONT . . ." and so on. This was done with much eye-rolling and a few burlesque bumps and grinds. While the performance was wildly received from the audience, the entertainer had neither much of a voice nor much personality other than the two outstanding projections.

A headwaiter led them toward an empty table. On the way, Francis, who had adopted his gayest manner, even to a slightly mincing step, loudly remarked:

"My Gawd, dearies! There's nothing like this in Philadelphia." Then, he pointedly asked their guide if this went on all night.

"No, sir." The headwaiter gave an understanding smirk, and an appreciative glance at the embarrassed Tiger. "We stop the service at two o'clock, though sometimes they just sit and camp until three or four," he gushingly confided.

"Well!" exclaimed Francis. "We're out to make a night of it." He slipped the man a folded bill, and added, "Though I would like to meet some of the local girls."

The attendant acknowledged the tip with a smile and said, "Perhaps we can fix that for you, too."

As their orders were taken, Francis and Tiger looked the place over carefully. A cleared space at one side and along the wall seemed to lead to several side doors. Three of these, in a row, were spotlighted, and labeled, 'Men,' 'Women,' and 'Us.'

Francis pointed out some other less conspicuous doors to Tiger, remarking that he was curious as to where they might lead.

After disposing of several drinks, and being entertained by further gaudy impersonators, none of whom were particularly amusing, Tiger arose, excusing himself. Francis quickly suggested that he might blunder into one of the unmarked doors to see what he could see. With a nod, Olsen weaved off through the crowded tables to the men's room, attracting many roving eyes as he went.

Several persons spoke, casually inviting him to sit down for a drink. Some, suggested other bolder things. Grinning fatuously and shaking his head, Olsen kept on his way. One or two interested men evidently decided that they should powder their noses just at this time, and followed the big man closely. Because of these, Tiger was forced to turn directly into the washroom, where he hastily locked himself in a cubicle. His thoughts, as he paused there, were mixed. In a way—this was all very funny. Laughable, at least.

And then he thought of Vivien. It occurred to him suddenly that she didn't know of her brother's death, and the presentiment came clearly that he would probably be the one to tell her. With this gim prospect foremost in his mind, he ignored the appraising glances, leers, and tentative conversational bids that were directed at him when he left the cubicle. He washed his hands and stalked out of the men's room.

He inadvertently turned in the wrong direction, and passing one of the questioned doors, noticed that it was slightly ajar. Quickly making up his mind, he assumed a slightly drunken swagger and lunged into the lighted room. He was in an office. Moreover, an old acquaintance of his was behind the desk.

"Tiger! Where did you come from? And what are you doing in this joint? Didn't think you'd go for the boys," remarked the grinning man behind the desk.

Tiger flushed and then laughed defensively as he stammered, "So, this is where Joe Cannelli makes all his dough . . ."

He stared, with pseudo-drunkeness, about the spacious and well-appointed office. He noted that there were several other doors beside the one through which he had blundered. He thickened his speech a bit as he added, "Yeah, showing a pal from the Marines some of the town. He wanted to see everything. Your joint, Joe?"

"Well, I run it. I have some partners, though. We gotta lot of connections."

Rising, the heavy-set, foreign-looking club operator indicated a small well-stocked bar.

"How about a drink with me, Tiger?" As he mixed the suggested drinks, he asked casually, "This friend, anyone I should know?"

"Nah! This guy is, or was, just an old buddy. He's been living back East. Say, Joe, this is sure better liquor than we got out there."

Cannelli laughed. "It better be. It isn't cut."

Tiger laughed with him, and after another gulp of his drink, said, "I haven't seen this guy for some time. I always thought he was a little different. Anyway, I suppose we'll make a night of it. He says he wants to try everything from sarsaparilla to a shot in the arm."

"Huh! Sounds like an expensive night."

"Oh, this guy's loaded. Say, Joe, where are some really rugged joints where these guys go? I've been going with girls so long, I guess I don't really know my way around the town."

At the query, Cannelli's eyes narrowed warily, but a second later he answered, "Hell, I guess you know as many places as I do, Tiger. I would like to meet your friend, though. At least I can pass the word to the bartender to use the good whiskey. . . ."

With this exchange, the club operator quietly ushered Olsen out into the main room of the place. The band, accompanying a chorus number of all the 'girls' brayed loudly. The customers seemed equally as boisterous, possibly anticipating the approaching closing hour. With a friendly clap on the back, Cannelli sent Tiger on the way back to his table, remarking that he would probably see him later.

On reaching the table, Tiger found that two other men, both obviously what they were, had joined Francis.

"Well, dearie, what were you doing so long in there —or what was doing you?" demanded Francis gayly.

"Believe it or not," Tiger grinned, "I met an old friend and had a drink with him." He looked questioningly at the newcomers.

With a wave of his hand, Francis said, "Oh, just

two more of the local girls. And this is my own Tiger," he added for the strangers' benefit.

Tiger shook two moist, limp hands in succession, and was just seated, when one of them put a hand on his arm.

"Say, aren't you Tiger Olsen from the Marines?"

Tiger rather curtly acknowledged this, and shook off the hand. The gay one smirked and said loudly,

"Why! I remember when you came back! I saw the parade and everything! And I've got all sorts of cute pictures of you in your football suit. Too bad you weren't a track man. They photograph so much more interestingly. Anyway, I've got all these pictures of you in my scrapbook of dream men. You must come up to my place and see it."

Though carrying on a conversation with the other stranger, Francis missed none of this. He was amused at Tiger's flushed confusion. Fortunately, at this moment, Joe Cannelli came up to the table with a waiter bearing a round of drinks. He greeted Tiger again, and looked questioningly at the three seated with him.

"Just wanted to be sure that you got a round on the house, Tiger. We've got to treat these Eastern visitors right.

Tiger, hoping that the brevity of his introductions would be acceptable, said as casually as he could, "Francis —Joe Cannelli. He runs this place."

Francis rose and struck a feminine pose. Shaking hands, he quipped, "At least, Mr. Cannelli, I brought a man into the house."

Joe laughed at this and admitted that not too many

did come to the Bait Room. Turning again to Olsen, he spoke in a lowered voice, "When you leave here, your friend might like the Gourmand." At Tiger's puzzled look, he added, "It's an all night spot with plenty of kicks. Tell 'em I sent you."

Tiger nodded his thanks as the club operator walked away. One of the characters at the table said, "My, Tiger! You do know the most exciting people."

Tiger ignored him and leaned closer over the table so that Francis could hear him over the bedlam of the club.

"Joe runs this joint, and I explained that you were a stranger in town looking for a thrill. I guess he had to size you up first. He must figure we're okay, because he suggested we try the Gourmand, wherever that is."

Francis grinned and nodded his approbation. More loudly, he replied: "Let's find out."

Turning to one of the habitues, he asked, "What kind of a spot is the Gourmand, dear?"

The effeminate youth rolled his eyes and gasped, "Oh, Bessie! That's one of those all night places, open from midnight to six in the morning."

"Do they serve drinks that late?" put in Olsen.

"Gawd yes!" gayly informed the other man. "At a price! You can get anything in that joint from a piece of trade to a main line shot—if you've got the money."

His companion seemed to take a dimmer view, and interrupted to say, "Well, I don't think it's safe there. They drink all night, and smoke weed, and turn tricks all over the place. I tell you, May, it's just too damned gay! They're due to be raided any time."

By this time Francis had gotten the idea. Noticing that the crowd in the Bait Room was thinning out, he finished his drink, much of which he had already slopped under the table unnoticed.

"Let's all go there, then," he giggled. "The night's still young."

The strange pair looked at each other, and Francis hastily added, "Oh, come on, you two. The party's on me!"

One of the two still hesitated, then he said, "Oh dear, I'd love to, but my husband is around here somewhere. I'd better find him."

As if on cue, another nervous character swished up to the group at the table, and began upbraiding the speaker. This turned out to be the 'husband'. As soon as the invitation had been made clear to him, he too, with an interested survey of Tiger, was ready to go. With girlish and attention-getting cries of pleasure the party finally made its way out of the Bait Room.

Outside, many taxis were taking off the crowd that was now surging from the place. Tiger mentioned that he had his car, but that it would only hold two. Francis, who was obviously expected to finance the trip, waved at a cab, and sent Tiger off to the parking lot with the admirer who kept a scrap book.

Some twenty minutes or so later, Tiger pulled up to the curb before a dingy building on a dark street in a slum section. Francis and his two companions were waiting at the door to the place. Tiger was now alone, and at Francis' amused query, he explained.

"That's just a great big mixed-up kid. He got awfully sleepy all of a sudden and had to go home."

Francis, noting that Tiger massaged a slightly reddened knuckle, laughed, and said, "Oh, you rough thing!" Then they turned to the dim doorway of the Gourmand Club.

CHAPTER TWELVE

Leaving his office after some final discussion with Captain Morphy and the government agent, Captain Starr turned in at Flanagan's for a nightcap. He anticipated the peace and quiet of the Back Room. He was a little surprised to find Senator Martin there. The senator greeted him casually and said something about waiting for a phone call.

The socialite, who never had been particularly friendly with the police officer, had obviously been at some dressy function; also, he suddenly seemed unusually affable.

After the waiter had brought drinks, Martin commented on the newest features of the three murders, which were emblazoned in the headlines of all the late editions.

"Captain, you do seem to have problems these days. Or, are these affairs Captain Morphy's problem?"

Starr glanced around to make sure that they were alone.

"No, these are mine. Though because of the characters involved, Morphy's as well as the other outfits, all have an interest."

"That's interesting, Starr. Though from all I could see with only a glance at the headlines, this is just a series of killings."

The police officer sighed. "I wish it were that simple, but there seems to be vice, bunco, blackmail, and other things besides homicide."

The elderly man grimaced expressively.

"That really seems to be a complete calendar of misdeeds. 'Other things'—humph!" he mused as if to half himself. Then he smiled as he remarked with the merest suggestion of sarcasm. "I suppose that actually these 'other things' include driving in the wrong lane, or overtime parking?"

Captain Starr rather heatedly replied, "As a matter of fact, Senator, the 'other things' involve a very widespread distribution of narcotics."

"Oh," said Martin, registering proper appreciation, "but I suppose you people will have it run down within a day or so."

Captain Starr was tired, and in consequence gave his answer slight consideration.

"I hope so! We do have several leads. Say, Senator!

You know a lot of people. Are you acquainted with a brother and sister by the name of Holden? They live out your way. I believe that their parents both died some years ago. And I think that these people own considerable property."

After a moment's thought, the older man nodded. "Yes, I think that I've met an Arthur Holden, and I believe that he does have a sister. How in the world do they fit into this thing?"

"Well, it's this third man that was killed. His sister mentioned this evening that her brother kept a diary, and when we get hold of it tomorrow, we just may find something in it that will lead us to whoever murdered these three men."

"I see," said the senator, "But why, if this is such an important lead, are you waiting for tomorrow?"

Captain Starr grinned involuntarily at Martin's stiff manner.

"You see, sir, his sister hasn't been told as yet that Arthur Holden is dead. So when we sent her home to get the diary she thought only that he was 'missing'. Part of our plan at that time was to delay telling her or publicly identifying the victim. But somehow it seems to have leaked the papers. So we'll wait until tomorrow to pick up the diary, if there really is one."

"Hmmm! Yes, I suppose that I do see it. All very complicated, isn't it? Well, Captain, it doesn't look like my party will call, so perhaps I'd better be getting along. Best of luck in running down your man."

With a sudden return to his customary caution, Captain Starr realized that he had said much more than he had intended. Of course, anything was all right with the senator, still he said, "Uh, Senator, I'd appreciate it if what I've said went no further for the time being."

Adjusting his homburg and smiling jovially, Martin clasped Starr's hand briefly.

"But of course, Captain!" he assured. "I must really be getting along. Goodnight! I shall see you soon, perhaps."

"Goodnight, sir," replied the tired Captain, who was really wondering whether he should have another drink or to get up and go home also.

The eye inspecting the party through the hole in the door of the Gourmand Club was cold and uninterested until Tiger mentioned that Joe Cannelli had sent them.

Their guide's manner was now effusive as they passed down a narrow, poorly lighted hallway. Francis' guests had expressed a desire to be called Frankie and Johnnie, though it was not clear in Tiger's mind which was which. They laughingly remarked of their guide, "Get her, she's tee'd to the ears."

The party was lead into a darkened room. After becoming accustomed to the dim light provided by a single enormous candle set in some sort of holder in the middle of the room and the few other small candles winking in the fringing darkness, they could make out a surrounding ring of upholstered booths. Some of these had curtains drawn before them, but those that were open ap-

103

peared to be filled with people who were drinking and laughing and obviously enjoying themselves in a normal cocktail-lounge fashion. An unseen pianist somewhere in the murky background was playing boogie on an instrument that sounded bizarre and out of tune.

Their guide installed them in a booth. When they were seated he asked what they would have.

There was, Tiger noted, a slightly dazed expression on this character's face. He seemed to speak jerkily as if his sense of timing were not functioning. But Olsen did not pay too much attention. Momentarily, his interest was arrested by a sight across the room as a curtain billowed away from a booth on a sudden current of air. What took Tiger's eye was not an illusion. Two service men, in uniform, were wrapped together in a desperately passionate embrace. These two, locked together lip to lip and hip to hip, were completely oblivious of all around them.

Oldsen nudged Francis. "Hey, get a load of that action."

Not only Francis stared at the straining couple, but Frankie and Johnnie and the waiter did also.

"Well!" exclaimed Francis emphatically, "the birds and the bees. Don't those two ever come up for air?"

The house character laughed shrilly at this. "Get you, May! You shoulda seen those two an hour ago when they got started. Hell! now that they're back up on their feet and buttoned up, they're just saying goodnight."

Tiger shook his head, and muttered, "Helluva long goodnight."

"Oh," smirked the waiter, "they been blasting, two

104

or three sticks a piece, and now they've got nothing but time. Say," he said, suddenly recalling that business came first, "you girls didn't bring a bottle, so what d'ya want?"

Tiger hesitated. Finally Francis spoke up. "Well, dearie, Cannelli said we could really have us a gay time here, so better make it the works."

"Yeah," naively put in Tiger, "let's have some drinks."

"Okay," said the waiter, and as Frankie and Johnnie nodded, he added, "Spose I might as well save a trip. What else d'ya need?"

Noting a hesitation, he laughed and added gayly, "Come on, girls! Let's live it up! A few sticks, maybe—or do ya want a fix?"

One of his 'guests' turned eagerly to Francis: "Let's blast a few, dear. Okay?"

Francis nodded in agreement, as if he was just getting the idea.

"Make it the works, Kate. A bottle of Scotch, and about a dozen sticks. We'll see where that gets us."

The waiter laughed shrilly and flounced off into the flickering shadows.

Tiger looked around. There was another ring of booths behind the one in which they were seated. These larger booths were also filled with people of all races and colors, more or less similar to the brassy crowd in the Bait Room.

There were only one or two women present, Tiger realized quickly, as his eye fell on one who sat back in the corner of one of those distant compartments. In the distance, the details were not too clear. If it had not been for the fact that all of the girl above the table was completely nude, he might not even have noticed her. Lounging beside her was a burly masculine type, who was sprawled partially across the table, one hand tentatively fondling the large breasts of the first.

Olsen was naturally interested and he continued to watch as this person removed his glasses, which he placed carefully on the table. Then put his cigar in an ashtray; and letting his fingers trail over and down and under the protruding flesh, he was suddenly lost to view as he buried his head in the girl's lap.

The lady smoked on unconcernedly, staring with complete indifference into nothingness. Only a slightly rhythmic jerking of her outstanding breasts indicated that she was alive.

"Get that fish queen!" simpered Johnnie, in patient disgust.

His friend smirkingly agreed with him: "Gawd, yes! Things like that give us honest girls a bad name."

At this point the waiter returned and unceremoniously dumped a bottle on the table. This was labelled 'Scotch Whisky'; and in consideration of the fact that the party had been sent by Joe Cannelli, it probably had a considerable percentage of that delightful beverage in it. Also plopped down were a bowl of ice, some glasses, and a short stubby section of candle similar to those they had noticed in other booths. Fishing in a pocket, the waiter brought out an opened pack of cigarettes of a popular brand. This last item he did not quite let out of his hands, as he blithely said,

"That'll be thirty dollars, dearie . . ."

Tiger started to explode in indignation, but Francis stepped on his toe and gripped his arm as he got out his wallet. Counting out the money, he thanked the waiter, and suggested that he return later.

At a nod from Francis, the two friends reached for the cigarettes. They quickly removed a couple of ordinary smokes from the pack. As one lit the stub of candle, the other took out of the pack two smaller, hand-rolled cigarettes. These were slightly shorter than the pack's usual content. Tiger noticed that the ends of these cigarettes had been carefully tucked in so as to preserve every shred of the 'tobacco'.

Francis warily watched this procedure while quickly pouring and downing several drinks from the bottle. As the two gleefully lit each other's cigarettes Francis whispered to Tiger, "Take it easy with that weed. We've got work to do."

By now Frankie and Johnnie had taken long deep drags on their smokes and were happily holding the fumes as deeply as possible in their lungs. As one exhaled reluctantly, the smoke was accompanied by a little giggle. This caused the other to laugh aloud—and this set the pattern for the next hour.

As Francis very obviously did not care to indulge, he had excused himself, indicating the whiskey and saying gayly, "I'd love to, girls. But you know, they really don't mix."

After a time, the waiter passed by and stopped to chat with Francis.

Tiger felt a bit 'out' of it all, so he casually picked

up one of the smokes the pair next to him found so enjoyable. Preparing it as they had, he soon had it alight and inhaled deeply. At the expression on his face, as the bitter acrid smoke bit into his throat and lungs, Frankie and Johnnie shrieked in merry amusement; Francis frowned.

This last was noticed by the observant waiter, who laughingly remarked, "Start 'em young, I always say! Anyway, dearie, he'll be just too weak to resist after a couple of those."

Francis laughed, but Tiger, who had over-heard the remark and understood its meaning, leaned forward belligerently, growling, "Listen, Buster . . ."

At this the houseman again laughed, though he edged away from the table and out of reach.

"Get you, doll!" he teased. "Buster isn't here tonight. Probably at the Baths. But I'm sure that you and he should meet."

Noting Francis' interested expression, which had been alerted at the mention of the 'baths', the waiter explained: "Buster is our trouble shooter and part-time bouncer, though he does seem to work more at the baths, lately. Anyway, he's about this one's size and type. I'll bet they'd do it real pretty."

Here Johnnie broke into the conversation. "You can have that one, dearie. He plays too damned rough! Did you hear about that belle he beat up—and knocked out one of her eyes?"

"Yes," agreed the waiter, helping himself to a drink, "But that's the way it goes, girl. We all get our kicks in different ways. Buster is really a nice guy. But I'll admit, he does play rough."

108

Frankie blurted out, "You'll never convince me that Buster didn't have something to do with that Kay! Why, they were shacked up together."

The waiter leaned over the table ominously, and catching Frankie's arm, said, "Listen, doll, we don't talk about Kay around here." Turning to Francis and Tiger, he gayly explained, "Some snotty young queen who used to hang around here shot herself with another guy. They were lovers, I guess." Shrugging his shoulders and downing another drink, the waiter swished away from the table.

Tiger, incoherently, started to ask something of Francis, but his query dwindled off into nothingness. Through it, however, Francis just barely overheard Frankie mutter, evidently speaking of the waiter, "Get that one! Took over Kay's job, maybe Buster, too."

And, to this Johnnie replied, "Yeah. Don't think I'd like to be in her shoes."

Almost an hour later, Frankie and Johnnie found an acquaintance, a type called 'Polly', who joined the party. All three were busy with their smokes, tittering and laughing merrily and inanely. Francis had been listening for any further reference to Kay, and had been steadily pouring drinks for himself. When unobserved, he'd pour these drinks on the floor under the table.

When Tiger had picked up a second of the handmade cigarettes, Francis had firmly taken it out of his hand. The big ex-athlete seemed happily acquiescent, though he had also begun to giggle slightly. Francis realized that it was time to make another move.

"My God!" he gasped, fanning the air about him, "It's too damned hot in here."

The marijuana smokers laughed hilariously at this, and the newest addition said, "Well, dear, let's go somewhere else."

This was just the opening that Francis had been waiting for.

"Okay, girls. But where'll we go at this time of the night?" and he went on, "remember, I'm a stranger in town."

Frankie said, "Let's go down to the square and get some trade."

Polly promptly vetoed this suggestion. "Oh, you and your hustling trade! They're all shop-worn anyway."

Johnnie, suddenly inspired, cried, "Girls! I know! Let's go to the Baths."

The late arrival, being more practical or possibly less high, asked, "That's an idea, but can we afford it?"

Johnnie volunteered, "Oh, its not so expensive, if you don't go in for those fancy deals upstairs."

Francis stood up and, motioning to Tiger who was resting easily with his head on the table, said, "Come on, kids. I've got some money left. Besides, you'll have to help me with this one. It looks like I'm going to have to steam him up a bit."

As they assisted Tiger to his feet, Francis realized that his big assistant was quite drunk. He hoped, however, that a lot of this was for the benefit of the others. Outside the Gourmand, the cold, fog-laden air cleared Francis' head. It didn't seem to affect the others, who chatted gayly as they waited to flag down a passing cab. Finally a cab appeared and they all crowded into it, with

110

Tiger safely between Francis and the driver.

"Where to, Mac?" asked the hacker.

"Let me see," said Francis, turning to the three in the rear, who merrily supplied the address. "But wait a minute," Francis added as the driver started to get under way. "You've got a radio, call the dispatcher and have him send out an extra driver, someone who can handle a Jaguar." He indicated the small sportcar at the near curb.

Within a very few minutes, another cab pulled up, and an extra man was given the keys which Francis had taken from Tiger's pockets. The cab drivers carefully compared the car registration with Olsen's identifications, and agreed to take the sportcar into the company garage until he should call for it. This, it seemed, was a customary service.

When this transaction was completed, Francis leaned tiredly back in the small part of the seat that the sleeping Olsen left unoccupied.

"Okay," he caroled gayly, "off to the baths, girls. Come who may. . . ."

CHAPTER THIRTEEN

The Baths were situated in an old but respectable looking building in the section of the city that had been rezoned for what was locally called 'the trade'. The building had actually come into existence some years before as the handsome annex to a school for young misses.

On the demise of this academy and up to the more recent cutting of a freeway through the property just to the rear of the building, the structure was variously used and abused until finally it had inconspicuously put forth a small and tasteful neon sign—"Baths".

After paying off the taxi and unloading the complacently agreeable Olsen, Francis stopped his little party at the entrance to the baths.

"Just what is the setup in here, dear?" he asked of Polly.

"Well, it's three dollars each to get in," said that one, happy to be an authority on something, "and you check your jewels and wallet and stuff at the desk." Here Polly leered. "And, of course, if you want any of the 'special features' you'd better carry a few dollars in with you. Then you register, just like for a hotel. They give you a skimpy towel and you go on back to those little rooms. Of course, all the girls call 'em cribs! Then you put all your clothes in the locker in your room and then you drape a towel around your hips and come out and cruise."

"Where's the 'bath' come in?" demanded the Tiger, suddenly alive.

"Oh you! You'll never get to it! There are a couple of showers at the back, and a sort of steam room and toilets and stuff. But most everyone just cruises around. If you see an open door, and someone interesting is inside, you go on in."

The large ex-Marine yawned and muttered, "Yeah. Well I just want to crap out in the sack for a couple of hours."

Johnnie said, "You'd better close your door tight, then, handsome or you're due for a helluva lot of company."

Tiger glanced at Francis who blushed becomingly, slyly winked and said, "I've already got a lot of company."

113

Francis asked, "What's this about 'special features'?"

"Oh," said the verbose Polly, "that's mostly for the rich old aunties, and bats like that. You have to go upstairs. They have some special 'masseurs' up there—at stud! Then, they have shows and exhibitions; but it runs into money. I've never been up there lately."

"That's where that Kay used to work, or she said she did, anyway. Besides, that Buster, he lives up there, I think," offered Frankie.

"That one!" exclaimed Johnnie. "He's too rough for me. He beat up a girl at the Gourmand one night when he was high, and they had to take her to the hospital. He's crazy when he's loaded."

"Did you get that waiter back there? She got all excited when we mentioned Kay. I guess that's Buster's new friend. But she can have my share," added Polly. To Francis he continued, "Anyway, dear, you should worry about going upstairs. You've got all you need right with you." This last was accompanied by a leer in Tiger's direction.

Francis was a little worried by these tentative overtures, not having any idea just how Olsen might react. He quickly let the group inside.

A little while later, after the party had been 'processed', they once again got together in one of the narrow hallways that ran between the tiny rooms. Each was clothed now only in a narrow towel draped jauntily or otherwise around the middle. The only other item of apparel was the key on a heavy rubber band. The three who had been there before wore this around the upper

114

arm like a bracelet. Fingering his own before he slipped it onto his arm, Francis was soberly reminded of a similar key he had examined some hours before in the morgue.

There was considerable 'traffic' cruising past the group. Most of these were middle-aged men, all of whom stared unabashedly at the muscular bodies of Tiger and Francis. A few exchanged greetings with Polly, Frankie and Johnnie. These three in due course drifted away on pursuits of their own. Francis and Tiger lounged tiredly in a doorway. For a few minutes, they quietly compared notes.

"Well, muscles, it's been a long day, hasn't it?" grinned Francis.

"Boss," groaned Tiger, who was actually not as knocked-out as he appeared to be, "you said the work would be different. But how different can it get?"

"Okay, fella. Keep your chin up."

"That's about all I could get up this morning," cracked Olsen.

Looking down the passageway behind Tiger, Francis noted an elderly 'bather' who had prowled past them several times. He was now talking to a very tall, skinny attendant dressed in whites. As Francis or Tiger seemed to be the subject of the conversation, Francis was not too surprised when they were presently approached by the man in white.

"Hello, you two," he greeted them with the same girlish effusiveness that seemed characteristic of all the people they'd met during the night. "Are you having fun?"

Tiger grinned drunkenly, and Francis quickly said, "Dearie, we've had it. Do you run this place?"

"Well, I'm sort of the Madam. Stepladder Kate, the boys call me." Looking about cautiously, he came closer and in a lowered voice continued, "Would you two like to make a little money this morning?"

"Doing what?" cautiously asked Francis.

"Well, dearie, you see, it's like this. I know that you two are new here. And that's what we like to see—fresh faces," he said with a glance at Tiger's draped mid-section. "Polly says that you're okay, and so do the others . . ."

"Come on, girl. Get with it," prompted Francis.

"Oh, okay! You see, we've got a lot of customers that like to see exhibitions. You know what I mean?"

Tiger looked a bit bewildered, but Francis nodded that he understood. The 'Madame' continued, "Now you two are a real pretty couple. Yes," he enthused, looking them over closely, "real pretty!"

Francis noticed one of Tiger's fists clenching, and he quickly intervened, demanding a cigarette and a light, which the character supplied. Francis remarked, "All right, dearie. We're on our honeymoon, so what's with it?"

"Well, we have a room upstairs, and it's really very nicely furnished. There's a big comfortable bed and—well, it's real nice, see. Then there are rooms on both sides, and people can look into the middle room without being seen. So, we put on some real gay parties for them to watch, and stuff like that."

"Yeah, sounds real cozy," offered Francis, "but where do we come in?"

"Oh, that. There's an old bat who would like to watch you and this one play. So if you'd like to make a few bucks, and enjoy yourself comfortably while doing it—"

"Aaah!" Tiger said disgustedly.

"No," said Francis. "I'm not sure that we have any play left this morning. Some other time, maybe."

Noticing that Tiger's attention was momentarily on two men down the passageway who had removed their towels and were appraising each other's charms, Stepladder Kate motioned Francis a few feet to one side.

"Listen, do you think that your friend would just pose, alone and stripped, like the ones they have in those muscle magazines? Real harmless stuff."

"Alone? All by himself?" asked Francis, wondering if this was a lead to what they sought.

"This old guy's real hot, and he's got plenty of loot!" said Kate.

"What kind of pictures?"

"Oh, just the usual 'art poses' like they sell in the books."

"Alone?" asked Francis, quickly turning over in his mind the advisability of going further with this.

"Why certainly! There'd be nobody except Buster in the studio with him. Buster's the photographer."

The name alerted Francis at once, though he maintained a show of disinterest. "No playing around?"

"For God's sake, Bessie! Are you afraid someone'll steal his cherry? Of course he'll be alone, except for Buster —and the pictures."

"Hey, what do you mean, 'Buster and the pictures'?"

Kate laughed shrilly.

"Oh! that's part of the gag, dearie! Y'see, we get a lot of reluctant fellows who are real pretty, like this one; but finally, for a few dollars, they will pose alone. So, Buster gets 'em on the model stand, and while he 'adjusts' the camera some sidelights go on that light up some big 'action' pictures that are right in front of the model. Well! these are some shots of some of the parties we have had up there. And believe me, my dear, they are real active! You can imagine what looking at them for a few minutes will do to the bashful model. Some of these old guys will pay real good for prints of that kind. Listen, Bess, if you can get handsome there to pose, I'll get Buster to save you some copies for your scrap book."

"Yeah, I see what you mean," said Francis, whose mind was busily considering all the possibilities. "Well, I'm tired. But maybe I can talk him into it. One thing; he's new at all this, so nobody had better get too close or bother him, because I think he'd get real rough. Okay?"

"Oh you! Certainly it'll be okay! Did you say that you were new here in Bay City?"

"Why, yes. But I've got a lot of friends."

"You must have, May! They called and okayed you from the Gourmand—said that you were friends of Joe . . ."

"Joe?"

"Sure, girl. Joe Cannelli—"

"Oh, that one! Well, as a matter of fact, they're all friends of Tiger. That's the lug with me."

"I see. He sorta reminds me of someone, but I just

118

can't remember who. Oh, well! Wishful thinking, I guess."

Francis turned back toward his assistant, "I'll see what I can do about that, but—" He shook his head doubtfully, indicating the big, stripped ex-marine.

"Okay," said Kate. "I'll be in front here by the stairs."

Francis joined Tiger who was grinningly engrossed with the two men farther down the passageway.

Francis nudged Olsen into a room and closed the door.

"I'm a son of a bitch!" exclaimed the ex-athlete. "I thought I saw everything in the Marine Corps. But if anybody had told me there were joints like this in my own home town—Hey, boss, let's clean house."

"Uh'uh, Tiger. Now listen to me a minute. I think I've got all that we came for, information anyway. But, I'd like to know about those private rooms upstairs.

He quickly explained all that had been told him by the houseman, and the offer that had come with it.

"Now, look, Tiger, I can't coldbloodedly ask you to do this. But it would sure help us. If you would only agree to pose, and then get up there and just stall. I don't think it would be a good idea to let this gang get any pictures of you stripped, though a nice big enlargement would made a dandy ornament on the wall over Hattie's desk. I'd like to get upstairs, and this might be our chance. As I see it now, these pictures could be at the bottom of the blackmail racket, but I'm not sure. You could size up the layout, and after you go up I'll try to follow you.

Maybe we could both get a look around. So, what do you say?"

"Oh, hell! said the tired Tiger. "Anything for dear old alma agency. But if some bastard gets too busy, I'm gonna slug him."

"Sure, sure, Tiger. But try to keep it down. Remember, we gotta get out of here, and our clothes and stuff are in the office. This ought not to take more than half an hour, and then we can go home and get some sleep. Boy, I'm pooped!" yawned Francis.

Tiger grinned. "Yeah! You're pooped. Get me!"

He turned and, hitching his towel more securely about his lean hips, left the cubicle and headed for the stairs.

CHAPTER FOURTEEN

The baths manager led Tiger up the stairs to the next floor. Stairs, Tiger noted, also continued to the third story, and a side stairway descended as well. As nearly as Olsen could recall the outside aspects of the building, these probably led to the parking lot side, where there was probably another entrance.

Kate ushered Tiger into a fairly large room, whose only discernible furniture was a great, low bed. This was opulently covered with some dark fur-like material, and was handily furnished with half a dozen paste colored pillows and cushions. As Tiger looked about him, the 'Madame' said,

121

"It's a gorgeous workbench, isn't it? Like something out of DeMille! And if it could talk! The mad affairs that have taken place on that couch . . ."

Olsen continued to look about the exotic room as this prattle continued. In a corner was a small raised platform with a classic-styled broken pillar on it. Across the room, situated so that it was in easy range of either the bed or the model stand, was a large complicated camera on a tripod. This was only partly hidden by a movable, folding screen.

On close inspection, Tiger noted that a wide frieze ran around the room just at eye-level. Stepping nearer, this was revealed as a series of enlarged 'action pictures' of men and women in various poses and positions. Even the detail, seen at a glance, brought a blush to Tiger's countenance. Obviously most of the pictures had been taken in this room on and about the great 'work-bench'. It was also apparent that this band of art studies could be lighted up when needed to inspire other models.

Short curtains were drawn across wide spaces in each side wall. One, slightly parted, revealed a mirror beneath. Tiger became aware that his guide was still talking.

". . . and so if you'll just wait here for a few minutes . . . Buster has probably gone upstairs. I think I heard his phone ring . . ."

"Who's Buster?" growled the tired Tiger.

"Oh, Buster's the photographer," Kate explained, and, suddenly aware of Olsen's obvious truculence, added, "He's also the bouncer. That is, he takes care of any trouble we might have in the house."

122

The veiled but implied threat of this last brought a grin to Tiger's face. "Well, okay. Unleash the dogs."

Nose in the air, Stepladder Kate flounced out. The door closed behind him with a decided click. Tiger at once tried it and found that he was locked in.

Broadminded as Tiger had been up to this point, he was definitely unhappy about the locked door. Feeling the panel over, he at once realized that it was well reinforced. A very angry ex-captain of Marines stood in the center of the 'party room', weighing possibilities.

Swift thoughts of demolishment and mayhem were quickly dispelled as the door opened and an elderly, distinguished looking gentleman entered. Before he could close the open door behind him, Tiger pushed him rudely aside, and propped the portal completely open with the corner of a heavy screen. Turning to his visitor, Tiger angrily demanded, "Are you Buster?"

"Heavens no!" was the amused reply. "Buster is more your size and type. Say! I know you! You're Tiger Olsen!"

"Yeah? So what?"

"Why, er—nothing, except that I remember you well. My! what are you doing here?"

"Listen, Mister! I'm just a tourist, see! Not that it's anybody's goddamned business what I'm doing here. What goes on here? And how come that door got locked?"

This all came out explosively as Tiger, fists clenched at his sides, stood belligerently over the older man, who now lolled back across the bed.

"Oh, come on, Olsen, simmer down. Nobody's going to hurt you. I saw that you were annoyed when Kate went out and locked you in, so I came over before you could wreck the joint."

"How do you mean—you 'saw' me?"

The man rose and walked to one of the draped sidewalls. There he pulled back the curtains to either side, revealing a simple, large plate glass mirror. Turning to the puzzled Olsen, he explained, "These are really tricky. They are mirrors on this side, but you can see through them just as if they were windows from the other side. That's why they have them here on both sides of the 'party room'. The spectators are in the rooms at either side. Then, too, this whole place is wired for sound. I heard Kate say that she was going to get Buster."

"Well, I'll be damned!" said Olsen. "Look, I'm sorry if I got sore. I guess I'm just tired. We've had a helluva night, and then some old bastard wanted us to pose for some pictures . . ." Tiger stopped, flushing with a sudden perception.

"Yeah, Tiger. I'm the old bastard. I guess I'm too old to play games anymore, but I do get a bang out of watching. Besides, I have an amazing collection of pictures. I certainly never thought I'd get one of Tiger Olsen. If Bruce hears about this, he'll raise the prices."

"Well, if that picture snapper don't get here pretty quick, I'm going home. Say, you don't seem like such— well, I mean, that is—you're not silly like those assholes downstairs."

"Thanks, Tiger. And you don't seem wise yet that

124

you shouldn't be in a place like this. As a matter of fact, if you'll take a tip from me, you'll get the hell out of here and stay away. There are some pretty rotten things in this setup." The gentleman stopped talking as Francis appeared in the doorway.

"Well, Tiger! Where did you get to? Need any help?" asked Francis, not quite sure of the situation.

"No. Everything's okay here, except that I'm supposed to be waiting for that tall guy."

At this, the 'Madame' appeared behind Francis, apparently very nervous or excited about something. His voice was unusually shrill.

"Ladies! What goes on here—a daisy chain? Buster was called away very urgently, and I must close off these upper floors. So, we'll just have to forget our little arrangement, and get our pictures some other time."

With a running-fire of this sort of chatter, he quickly ushered the three men downstairs, where the distinguished old man lingeringly clasped Tiger's hand in parting.

Tiger and Francis went to their rooms to dress. Fifteen minutes later they were in a taxi, heading for home. It was 7:45 A.M.

CHAPTER FIFTEEN

Shortly after ten o'clock the same morning, Francis briskly entered the offices of the Morley Agency. He was greeted by a slightly acid Hattie.

"Banker's hours, eh, Mr. Morley?"

Francis stopped at his receptionist's desk. After a slight pause during which he rapidly counted to ten, answered smilingly,

"No, Hattie dear, not banker's hours. But, should you care, Bessie, Tiger and I were with the police on a triple murder the entire night. We got home at about eight, two hours ago. I for one had just time to change,

clean up, have coffee and get down here, to be nagged as
I come in the door. Now, if think that is a sufficient
resume of my night, we can proceed. What's doing?"

"Oh, well, I'm sorry, Mr. Morley, but it's been quite
a morning. Those decorators are in Mr. Olsen's office,
and there is some sort of hassle on about some 'off-pink'
drapes.

"I'm sure he'll adore off-pink."

"Yes! I can see what you mean. Then there have been
more applicants for the job. How is Mr. Olsen working
out?"

"Just peachy! Frankly, dear, I only hired him because
I could see that he was your type. And I do so want to
keep you happy."

"Oh, Mr. Morley . . ." The secretary blushed becomingly.

"Miss Campbell, I'm just a trifle unwell this morning. Now, please, stop twittering. Has anything important
come up?"

"I was just getting to this, sir!" snapped Hattie with
considerable hauteur, "Captain Starr has called several
times."

"Now that, toots, is more like it."

Francis turned to his own office. Just as he reached
the door to his private domain, he heard Hattie offer:

"If I felt that bad in the mornings, I'd do something
about it."

Francis paused and turned patiently, realizing that
his secretary was really only trying to be helpful in her
own way. "And what, dearie, aside from Lydia Pinkhams

or a whirling spray would you suggest?"

Hattie, mollied by Francis' seemingly receptive attitude, said brightly, "Mr. Morley, have you ever tried one of those Turkish baths?"

Francis stared at the woman in sheer amazement; then, mouthing a horrible groan, he fled into his own sanctuary, slamming the door behind him.

Hattie, at her desk, upright and slightly offended, spoke only to the wall calendar when she muttered, "Get her!"

After a quick Bromo, neatly chased by a large slug of Metaxa, a bottle of which he had thoughtfully laid in the day before for just such emergencies, Francis felt revived. He had barely got this potion down, and was considering writing a concise report of the night's activities, when the door burst open and in walked Captain Starr.

"Good morning, Captain? Take that chair over there."

After returning the greeting gruffly and seating himself, the homicide officer came abruptly to the point of his visit.

"Morley, I'm afraid that we all got a little carried away last night. That is, this seems to be a routine police matter. And after some consideration I don't think that the Department would care to be in the position of turning this thing over to a private agency."

Francis interrupted. "I can see your point, Captain Starr, but I thought that we were all agreed that speed was of the essence in this, and that acting unofficially I might be able to do what the known police could not."

"Well, yes. We did say that. But—"

Francis slid some loose papers across the desk.

"Perhaps you'd like to make some notes, Captain."

"What d'ya mean?"

"First, the narcotics." Francis leaned back in his chair, and then with a sudden inspiration he leaned forward and flicked a key. "Miss Campbell. Please put this on tape and transcribe it later, two copies. This is a summation of a report entailing conversation between myself and my assistant, Mr. Olsen. Do you understand, Hattie? There are just Olsen and myself present."

"I understand, Mr. Morley. This conversation of an agency report is informal and between you and Mr. Olsen. Okay, I've got it. Good morning, Captain."

Captain Starr started to respond to the greeting, but at a motion from Francis growled unintelligibly instead. Then he demanded,

"What's all this monkey business about?"

Francis switched the intercom off momentarily and replied, "I just thought that I could make a report for my files and possibly a copy for you as well. By using Olsen's name, Captain, we can keep anything official out of it. Now," he again switched the key to "ON":

"The narcotic angle," Francis began.

"Yeah" muttered Captain Starr skeptically.

"My assistant and I went to the Bait Room and there met personally a Mr. Joe Cannelli, the operator of that place."

"No!" exclaimed the police officer.

"We asked where something more lively might be obtained, and Cannelli sent us to a place called the Gourmand, also owned and operated by Cannelli. By now there were four in the party, all of whom will be available as witnesses. We were admitted at the Gourmand only because Cannelli had phoned and okayed us. This was just after two A.M., but we were offered and served whiskey. About a hundred other patrons were similarly served until about four-thirty A.M., when we left. We were offered and sold marijuana. At least two of my party used these cigarettes. Others about the place were openly using this narcotic, which was openly supplied by the waiter. The same waiter also offered a 'fix', or a short supply of cocaine. Other drugs including LSD and peyote were suggested as available. Cannelli seems to have an over-all control on this distribution. But between himself and the passer—that is, the waiter who made the actual sale—there is another character, whom we didn't see, named Buster."

Francis paused for breath, then continued:

"Another spot, where we were also okayed by Cannelli, was the 'Baths'. This would seem to tie up at least three joints with Mr. Cannelli, with dope sales in at least one and 'steerers' in the others. There are four witnesses to all of this activity. Now, does that tie up the narcotics angle?"

Open-mouthed, the police officer stared at Francis. Finally he shook his head as if in complete disbelief, and only remarked:

"I'm a son of a bitch!"

Francis nodded as if in complete agreement, and cheerily went on:

"Next, we have a blackmail pattern that seems to

130

lead to these deviate murders. We have located and personally inspected one setup around which all of this may
revolve. We found steerers in three or four deviate hangouts, all steering to the 'Baths'. This is a sort of boarding
house, self-service sex bargain counter for men only.
That is, it's a place men go for men who go for men,
if you follow me. The place has some very interesting
sidelines. A complete photographic studio does pictures
of various persons in various compromising positions.
These pictures may or may not be taken with the subject's
knowledge. There is every indication that this department
of the Baths is frequented by many gentlemen of means.
Now, here is an angle. The photographer is a guy named
Buster, the same one who more or less manages the Gourmand. His late assistant was Kay Dunbar; and there is a
definite rumor among the 'boys' that Kay got to know too
much and Buster disposed of him. The man is a muscular
masochist and confines his pleasures to young and attractive men. We know that whoever killed Dunbar also murdered at least two others. It could have been this Buster,
as far as our observations have told us; though we have
not yet seen the man."

Francis clicked off the intercom and leaned back in
his chair.

"Now, Captain," he said, "How's that for a night's
work on your 'police matter'?"

The veteran officer shook his head. "I don't get it! A
stranger in town, and, why we—"

Francis interrupted, "As I told you, I can get into
these places."

Leaning again over the desk set, Francis instructed

131

Hattie to make up two copies of the report, and then clear the tape. Turning to the homicide officer, he continued,

"If I might make a suggestion, Captain, your Captain Morphy of the vice squad gave us the names of several places last night, all 'gay' joints. There were five of these baths mentioned. Now, as I see it, the bars and clubs all have something to sell, something from which an ostensible profit may be legitimately derived. The baths on the other hand can only bring in a return in rentals, as far as the owners of the properties are concerned. I would suggest that someone find out who owns these five places. Very possibly they may be acquaintances or business associates of Joe Cannelli. There seems to be some sort of tie-in."

"As a matter of fact, Morley, I am an acquaintance of Joe Cannelli. A lot of people know him. He's supposed to be a gambler."

"Well," sighed Francis, "I suspect that he's gambling with lives right now."

"By the way," asked Starr, "did Tiger Olson get hold of that Holden diary?"

"Why, no—" Francis was interrupted by the buzzing of the intercom.

He answered this to hear Hattie ask:

"Is Captain Starr there? I have a very urgent call for him."

Francis handed the phone to Starr, who answered gruffly, and then listened with an excited interest. He hung up and got to his feet. Standing over Francis, he asked, "You're sure that you can back all this up?"

"Captain, I have said there were witnesses."

"Okay, okay. Now we've got another angle. They've kidnapped Vivien Holden."

"They've what?"

"Yeah. A couple of guys got to her apartment a little after seven this morning, tied her up and started searching. Then the maid came in, and they tied her up, too. They hunted everywhere, nearly wrecked the place. Then they took the Holden girl away."

"What in the world were they looking for?"

"A book of some kind. I've a feeling it might have been the diary."

"But, Captain, nobody knew about that. She only remembered it as she was leaving here late yesterday afternoon. But when he took her home, I guess they both forgot about it. At least that's what he said this morning. So who else knew about it?"

The police officer shook his head.

"It beats me! Didn't Olsen say anything about it at all?"

"Uh-uh, except that he had forgotten about it. Say, what time did you say—at seven this morning?"

Captain Starr nodded.

Francis considered for a minute, then said, "Well, I personally think that this all ties in with the Baths. Buster may have been the one that blackmailed and killed the Holden girl's brother. Now there comes up a mention of his having kept a diary. At seven in the morning kidnappers call on Vivien, the murdered man's sister, who might have the diary. Okay—" Francis paused as he saw where this cumulative reasoning was taking him.

Captain Starr said impatiently, "Yeah . . . ?"

133

"Well," continued Francis, "to my own personal knowledge, Buster was suddenly called away from a very profitable job of photography just before seven this morning. And, a half hour later, the manager of the Baths was clearing everyone out of the upper floors there. I'll bet—"

The detective officer snatched at the phone, but Francis stayed his arm. He looked unsmilingly into the officer's eyes.

"Yes, I think so too. I honestly believe that all they'll want from the girl is the diary, if there is one. Possibly some ransom money. I mean, I don't think that she's in any immediate danger. Now, I ask you to give me two hours. Tiger and I can easily get back in there, and we know the layout. And, Captain, after all, she's my client."

The policeman's hand relaxed on the telephone as he considered this. Finally he nodded. "Okay, it's eleven now. At one o'clock, we'll come into that joint—and strong! Meantime, do what you can."

As the officer turned to leave, Francis said, "Why don't you run down those property owners, Captain. And, oh, by the way, I just remembered something. Someone, somewhere last night said something about someone named Bruce. If there is such a person, he might be the big one."

Captain Starr stopped as if pole-axed. Without even turning around, he asked, "You're sure the name was Bruce?"

"Sure, I'm sure! Some old character at the baths made some crack about Bruce raising the prices. Why?"

134

"Bruce! I should have known better. The diary—"

"Say, Captain Starr, what's the matter?"

Francis reached into the desk drawer and took out a glass, with the bottle of pungent Greek brandy. He quickly poured a large measure and handed it to the homicide officer.

Starr, still standing like a man in shock, took the drink and downed it. He shuddered, and then, carefully setting the empty glass on the desk, turned again to the door. Here he paused, hand on the knob.

"Well, we'd better find her. I know now how they found about the diary. I told them."

With this cryptic remark, the police captain strode from the room, slamming the door behind him.

CHAPTER SIXTEEN

Francis parked the car hastily in an opening at the curb. The neighborhood was busier now at midday, though it was still an obvious back-wash of the busy city. He had quickly briefed Tiger on his concept of the situation, and between them they had come to an identical conclusion.

If this was where Vivien was being held—and both thought that it probably was—they were fairly sure that she would be kept on the more private upper floors. Also, they realized that they had little more than an hour, and it would take some time for them to get into the place in a natural way. This possibly halved their time in which to find the girl before the police arrived and broke it all up.

"Why don't we just let 'em do it?" asked Tiger.

Francis shook his head stubbornly.

"No, I've been thinking about this, and while it may seem like a pretty mercenary point of view, it's the way I feel about it. Y'see, Tiger, we've gotten mixed up in something pretty nasty here. If we help the police to break it all up, that's okay. But we, the Agency, have spent a lot of time and money getting this far. Now, as I see it, we've got a client, a customer. Vivien Holden. She hired us to find her brother. Well, we found him. As a matter of fact, we knew where he was, but he was dead. Now our investigation has got our client kidnapped. Okay, maybe we can get her out of there if she's still safe and sound. If we are right, we will have solved his murder at least. I think with this much accomplished we can send the young lady a bill without feeling too badly about it. After all, she's got the money. Well, what do you think, Olsen?"

Tiger hesitated, shaking his head grimly. "Hell! I don't know, Frank. I guess you're right. Well, hell, let's find her first."

Francis gave his assistant a long look, and then smiled easily. "Crazy, man! Come on, you big mass of muscles, let's do it!"

With this, they left the car and crossed the street to the Baths. As they entered, Tiger murmured, "Here we go again, boys . . ."

It was Francis' hope that the attendants who had seen them the night before would now have been replaced by a day shift, and in this they were lucky. Quickly registering, they told the blondined character at the desk that they wouldn't be in for long, and so wouldn't bother to check anything. This brought a knowing leer from the extrovert under the tied-and-dyed hair and a 'gay' remark suggesting procedure. The two hurried on into the long, cubicle-filled room.

The stairs to the upper floors were to the left. Kate had been relieved by another attendant who sprawled in a chair placed across the bottom step. The agency men proceeded with their hastily devised plan. Fortunately, their assigned 'rooms' were toward the rear.

Francis and Tiger quickly entered one of the little rooms, and at once started a scuffling noise which rapidly grew in volume. From without it could easily have sounded like a serious altercation or a fight. The plan worked like a charm, quickly bringing the attendant, who knocked forcefully on the door.

"Hey! What's going on in there? Can't you guys do it quietly?"

Francis moaned convincingly. Tiger, partly concealed behind the door, fumbled open the latch. Then from the rear of the little room, Francis moaned again, adding dramatically, "Oh, please come in and help me."

The attendant pushed the door open, and seeing only Francis cowering in the far corner with his arms about his head, he came on into the cubicle, asking very rudely, "What the hell's the matter with you, dearie?"

This was his last remark for some time. The Tiger gave him a simple judo cut behind the ear that dropped him unconscious at their feet. Francis quickly relieved him of the large bunch of keys that hung from his belt, and the limp attendant was shoved back under the narrow bed. Olsen gazed wonderingly at his open hand.

"Hey, Frank, I always wanted to see if that would work!"

"Silly boy! Come on, I've got the keys. We'll just walk quietly. Leave this one here. He'll keep."

They met no one on their way to the stairs, nor on the way up to the next floor. Here Francis whispered to Tiger, "I'll go on up to the third while you look through these rooms down here." At Olsen's nodded agreement, Francis continued on up the stairs.

Tiger turned to the nearest door, which led into one of the 'viewing' rooms, though he hardly recalled the exact layout here. The room he entered was dark, but Tiger could clearly hear sighs and moans, gasps for breath, and the faint creaking of a bed in use, all of which could only indicate that at least two people were struggling furiously in the dark. As he stood motionless listening, a sudden lift of one hand caused it to brush across a curtain of some sort. Tiger heard a faint tingle, like that of a ring on metal. The vibrant and passionate breathings of two people continued without interruption.

Somehow these faintly guttural noises reminded him him of something, or someone, but just what escaped him at the moment. Almost at once he realized that the unseen pair were not exactly fighting.

139

Suddenly Tiger remembered the two-way windows. He tried to recall whether they were curtained on both sides. Yeah! That old guy had said you could hear it all from next door as well as watch!

Carefully, Tiger ran his hands over the hanging material. Yes! these were short drapes that covered a glass pane. Finding their center, he cautiously drew them apart . . . and stood completely dumfounded by the picture that met his eyes.

One of the two sweaty bodies writhing in a posture of sex was clearly and dearly familiar to Tiger. The instant thought of rescue was quickly abandoned when he realized that here was no rape, no forceful taking of the woman who had been so quiescently pliant beneath him only a few hours before.

This was a maddened, abandoned, wild creature—moaning, clasping, biting, straining at the body that violently twisted and contorted itself with her own. Sweat broke out on Olsen's brow as, for a single instant, the two beyond the window seemed to pause at the very pinnacle of violence and motion. Vivien's lithe and perfect body, glisteningly drenched with perspiration, lay momentarily stretched out. Her head and shoulders were bent almost double. In its classic and momentary immobility her body might have been likened to a classic Grecian sculpture.

Complimenting this and equally as artistically attractive was the bronzed, powerful body of the man. His lower limbs were almost outstretched and his upper body was inversely twisted into a complimenting duplicate of her pose.

140

The two paused in their frenzied play as if to draw the last possible bit of passion and response from each other. Tiger's eyes noted the clothing, torn and flung to one side. He saw, too, a short-handled whip with knotted thongs of leather. Hurled down as if useless, were several small rattan canes. These and other objects that appeared to have been employed but briefly and then discarded were strewn about the floor near the great bed.

Tiger's questing eyes and alert mind took all this in, in a matter of seconds. His own features simultaneously blushed at the thoughts and memories his mind sent racing through his massive body. Even as he stared, the great muscled lover's body fell away from Vivien as though tired and deflated. His strong hands fumbled in her tousled hair, pulling her eager head away from his tired flesh.

The acoustics were so excellent that Tiger could hear a faint mouth sound as her lips were pulled away from the man. Even as he pulled her so that she lay half across him, the man reached roughly for one burgeoning breast, across which blood-streaked lines showed. Almost as a man admitting defeat, the tired eyes beneath the beetling brows met the girl's triumphant ones. She laughed drily, then joyously and victoriously.

In a moment, the man reached down, his huge biceps indicating his great power and strength as he pulled the girl's body up to and onto his own. For a moment he held her suspended above him, and then impulsively clasped her to him. Just the single note of another peal of mad laughter escaped her mouth before he caught and buried it and her lips between his own. Fiercely, roughly, he hugged her to him. To the unseen and unsensed observer, it seemed as if the man's passion would break her in two. Then, in another swift movement, he again held her away from himself and pantingly demanded, "Damn you! Where's the diary?"

Lightly, as if in the middle of an innocent social conversation, she jibed, "And you thought that you could hurt me! You've beaten me, whipped me, taken me roughly and painfully, and I've gone you better every time. It's you who are tired of it now, you who want to stop."

She laughed again. This time a note of scorn was apparent in her voice. Scorn, clear even to Olsen who could hardly believe that this wanton was the girl he had forcefully, manfully, but tenderly and naturally seduced a few hours before. Could this be the girl who had whimpered softly with passion as he had lain upon her?

Olsen shook his head to get the cobwebs of memory from it. As he watched, enthralled and almost unbelieving, Vivien pulled roughly away from the man beneath her and flung herself to one side of the great bed. One of her dainty hands reached out tentatively. With a disdainful fingertip, she flicked at the man.

"You can't hurt me, Buster, as big as you are." She laughed wildly.

For a moment the man lay inert beside her, then he jumped to his feet. He grabbed up a robe from the floor and shrugged into it. Walking around the bed, he stood over her. Even as he stood there, breathing deeply, his shaking shoulders indicated to Tiger his great anger and frustration. Vivien gazed up at him, smiling. She languidly raised her hands to part his robe.

With one huge hand he knocked hers aside; with the other he grabbed her by the hair. His rage was now obvious to the girl, and his efforts to contain his madness caused his entire body to shiver.

Pulling her up from the bed by her hair, he said, "I'll hurt you, you greedy bitch! I'll hurt you! I'll kill you! But before I do that I'll tell you something that will take the grin off that greedy mouth of yours. Yes, I'll tell you something that will really hurt you, and then I'll kill you! You won't be the first I've killed. Do you know who was the first? Yeah! Now I interest you, don't I? Well, I beat him, too, and whipped him, and did everything to him that I've done to you! And he liked it. He begged for more, and he paid money, too."

The hulking, hovering man, insane with his rage, shook the woman as if she were a rag doll. His voice was a shout of triumph as he went on,

"Yes, I said 'he'. Oh, he loved it, too! It must run in your rotten family. Sure, that's right. You're as perverted as he was! And so you want to be beaten some more, and whipped and used, do you? But I can't hurt you, you think! Well, I can kill you—just like I killed your precious brother."

A little scream came from Vivien, and for the first time in these seemingly endless minutes, Tiger saw pain and fright in the girl's eyes. She tried desperately to pull away as Buster grabbed her by the throat. Even as the big hands clasped themselves around her neck, Tiger

143

started towards the door he had blundered through only a few minutes before. Suddenly, an alarm bell sounded through the hall, loud and insistently.

Tiger's eyes turned back to the window in time to see a desperate Buster drop the girl and leap to the door of the party room. There he paused but a second. Tiger knew that he must have pressed some hidden button, because the door promptly swung wide. Buster ran quickly through, slamming it behind him.

As he watched, spellbound by all he had seen, Tiger saw the girl—again the sweet, frail creature he had met only yesterday afternoon—fall back crying on the great bed.

CHAPTER SEVENTEEN

On the floor above, Francis faced a long hallway with several closed doors on either side. A few ceiling lights burned dimly, and at the far end a window was unshaded but crudely painted over. Bright spears of light filtered through this rude blackout in spots where the paint had peeled away. On closer examination Francis saw that this window was also nailed shut. A glimpse through one of the scaling paint holes, showed only emptiness which reached down to the faintly heard noises of the traffic on the freeway far below.

Turning to the door, Francis tried the knob and was

not surprised to find it locked. The third key he used opened the door, admitting him to a dusty, meanly furnished office.

A small safe stood in one corner with its door ajar. A partly opened door revealed a closet that was bare except for some photographic supplies on the shelves. Another door was closed on a bare and utilitarian bathroom, whose principal piece of furniture was an old iron bathtub propped up on unbelievable claw feet. A moth-eaten sofa cowered against one wall of the office, and long heavy drapes concealed most of another. Drawn back, these disclosed a large window that looked out pleasantly over the sunlit city.

Francis spent little time with this handsome view, but quickly turned to the desk in the center of the room. Its top was littered with odd papers and a few photographs. These were at once apparent as products of the house photographer, and were certainly not meant for public viewing.

With a grunt of disgust, the Agency man tore these across and dropped them into a large metal utility wastebasket. With the glimmerings of an idea, he quickly added the hastily inspected letters and other papers from the desk top. One unlocked drawer yielded a bunch of small photos showing more natural activities and a small packet of booklets. The other drawers of the desk, which he quickly pried open, seemed to hold nothing of importance. All papers that he found were added to the mass in the basket. A bottle and some glasses were left as they were. Some small packets of folded paper that contained a white crystalline powder, he also left intact.

Crossing to the safe, Francis edged the heavy door open. He found a small but business-like file inside. Several reference books of the Who's-Who type, a city directory and some lists of names and addresses bound into pamphlets were also among the safe's contents. The pamphlets Francis assumed to be the usual professional sucker lists, and he thought that they might be of some future use. Pocketing these, he next found, to his considerable surprise, a heavy manila envelope containing a thick sheaf of currency. A quick glance showed a predominance of hundred dollar bills. Holding this in his hands for the briefest of moments, Francis considered that he was as honest as the next man and stuffed it away carefully in an inside pocket.

The letter file proved to be of even more interest. In alphabetical order were photos, letters, registration cards for the baths below, and in most cases small ledger sheets showing notations of various sums of money and appended with cryptic and undecipherable notes. Each grouping seemed to cover fully a period of visits to the Baths, then to the 'party' rooms, with detailed photos covering these later visits. The ledger notations undoubtedly listed the further tribute occasioned by these pictured visits.

There were over fifty individual files in the container. The photographs brought blushes even to Francis. He impulsively dumped the whole file and its contents into the waste container.

Francis began to realize that he had spent some time

in this one room and that there might be little enough time left to find the girl; nevertheless, he could not resist the impulse that made him pause, dry his gun down on the corner of the desk, gather up the loaded waste basket and carry it into the bathroom. Here he dumped everything into the huge iron tub and, with a flick of his lighter, set everything afire.

With a smile on his face, he stepped back into the office, closing the bathroom door behind him, just as the hall door burst open. A huge, disheveled and angry man rushed into the room, holding a dressing gown about his massively muscular torso.

Both men stopped for an instant. Then Francis, intent on edging toward the gun he had carelessly left on the desk, involuntarily glanced in that direction. This alerted the robed intruder, who bellowed, "Who the hell are you?" Without waiting for an answer, he leapt toward the weapon.

In his rush, Buster's head and shoulders protruded. Francis paused, seeing that he couldn't reach the gun first, and neatly but heavily drop-kicked the heavy chin. Buster's head snapped back and he stumbled, falling across one corner of the desk. The force of his fall knocked the gun to the floor, where it slid under the sofa.

As if in answer to the question put him, Francis, edging toward the door, replied, "I'm Morley, and you must be Buster."

The big man in the robe rose from the desk, shook his head and felt his jaw gingerly. Then, noting Francis' intention, he stalked across the room. As soon as he was near enough he launched a devastating blow at the calmer Agency man. Francis ducked this neatly and sidestepped, as he cooly demanded, "Where is the girl?"

Again trying to slug Francis, the burly photographer swore awesomely, but did reply, "That goddamned nympho! She's downstairs, and as soon as I get you, I'll take care of her . . ."

Francis again avoided a rush, though not completely. The edge of the heavily swung fist caught him alongside his ear. Even though Morley did not get the full power of the blow, his attacker was obviously both hurt and winded. It rocked him back and made him acutely aware of his immediate danger. The bull-like Buster set himself for another swing.

Francis coolly coordinated his own slighter body, allowing the sledge-like blow to pass close by his head. However, instead of backing away, he moved in swiftly and grasped the folds of his opponent's robe. With a secure grasp of the heavy fabric and a guiding elbow to the bigger man's hip, Francis dropped backwards to the floor, neatly kicking Buster's feet out from under him.

The fall and the big man's off-balance weight pivoted nicely against Francis' stiff arm in this elemental judo throw. The Agency man was pleased to feel his bulkier adversary swing up and over him.

Expecting to hear the released body land in a corner with a crashingly satisfactory thud, Francis was shocked at the noisy crash of breaking glass.

After a long, single second, he heard the fast receding scream of a man falling through space.

Turning on one knee, Francis saw that he was alone in the room. A draft of cool summer air came in through the shattered remnants of the big window.

Shaking his head to clear it from the single blow he had received, Francis retrieved his gun, and, pausing only to make sure the fire in the bathroom was burning nicely, fled from the office. In the hallway he heard shouts from below. The place had become a bedlam of noises.

Racing down the stairs, he met Tiger, who was half consoling, half supporting a very disheveled Vivien. She was partially wrapped in an oversized bedspread, and for all the urgency and seriousness of the occasion, Francis had the rather alien thought that she looked downright desirable. The bedspread, as large as it was, was doing little to cover certain important portions of her body. But this was no time to ponder the lovely mysteries of Vivien Holden.

A force of men was breaking into the building on the floor below. Francis made a split second decision. He indicated the stairs that led to the side door and shooed Tiger and Vivien quickly down them.

The three were across the street, into the car and away just before the block became completely entangled with arriving police cars, ambulances and fire equipment.

Driving quickly away from the building that now belched smoke and flames from the roof and one side, Francis' smile was more or less smug as he patted his full pockets. From the corner of his eye he saw Tiger the Rescuer patting something else equally as full.

150

CHAPTER EIGHTEEN

It was the next day, nearly noon. Tiger and Francis had again compared notes, after a complete review of the whole business with the police and a man from the District Attorney's office. They had finally dictated to Hattie a discreet report of what Francis would always feel would surely be the Agency's maddest case.

After reminding their girl-of-all work of the utmost secrecy and astounding her with a very generous check in four figures, Vivien Holden's contribution just prior to her sudden departure on an extended world cruise, Francis leaned back in the chair behind his desk.

"Well, muscles, now that you've rested, what do you think of our little Agency?"

"Huh! get her," Tiger grinned.

Francis interrupted, with a hint of annoyance in his eye.

"Just for the record, Mr. Olsen, let me do the camping in this act. I'll make with the gay talk. You just be big and beasty. Okay?"

The big, handsome ex-Marine sensed that his employer was not altogether joking, but he only had the opportunity to shrug an acknowledgement of this when the door opened and Captain Starr walked in.

Francis greeted him cordially: "Hello, Captain, say, don't you ever knock? Why, for all you know, Tiger and I might have in an embarrassing position."

"Knock it off, Morley," said the big detective officer, with a nod for Tiger as well. "I thought that we'd have one more little talk. And if there are any angles that we didn't get around to with the D.A. last evening, we could clear it up now."

The official flung a late paper on Francis' desk and slumped into a convenient chair and crossed his legs comfortably. Tiger noticed the small bandage on the palm of the Captain's hand and casually remarked,

"What happened to your hand, John? Cut y'self?"

The Captain flushed, but after a second he replied evenly and almost as casually, "Nope, got bit by a dog. Trying to give this pup some warm medicine, y'see, and he nipped my hand."

During this brief exchange, Francis had been scan-

152

ning the headlines which read, 'CITY MOURNS SEN-ATOR MARTIN". The lengthy and laudatory story that followed gave the highlights of Martin's career as a public official and leading citizen. Reading with only a partial interest, Francis noted that the body had been found by Captain of Detectives, John Starr, a close personal friend who had called socially on the Senator late on the preceding afternoon.

Raising his eyes from the newspaper, Francis met those of the police officer.

"Oh, Captain, so that's where you were late yesterday afternoon. 'Close personal friend' . . . well. I'm sorry, sir. Believe me."

"Did you know that Tiger knew him, too?" asked the Captain.

"We weren't really well acquainted, John," Tiger spoke up. "I used to see him around. Mostly at the Back Room."

"Well, gentlemen," said Francis, "You both have my sincere condolences. Tough, Captain, that you should walk in on his body."

Captain Starr nodded.

"Yes, I went to see Bruce Martin about a personal matter. Nothing important now. His houseboy was there, but he hadn't bothered to call the Senator, who kept pretty late hours and liked to sleep in the daytime. I guess he wasn't well. He had various medicines in bottles, on a table alongside his bed. Mostly plain ordinary stuff like aspirin and sleeping pills. But there was one bottle that was labeled 'poison'. This was some kind of potent heart stimulant. His doctor says that he was subject to mild attacks and that those pills were strictly for an emergency and never to be taken more than one at a time. It appears that he must have reached for the aspirins and somehow got the wrong bottle, taking three or four of the 'poison' tablets. At least, that's what the doctors all agree."

Francis had become very quiet during this almost unnecessary recital. After a pause, he remarked casually, "Definitely accidental, then?"

For a long moment, Starr's eyes met Morley's. There seemed to be present in the room a note of hovering tension.

Francis gazed steadily at the neat bandage on the police captain's upturned palm. Again his eyes met Starr's. After a long minute, Francis lowered his glance and reached for a cigarette. Lighting it, he mused, just audibly, "Bruce Martin . . . Bruce . . ."

Snapping his lighter shut decisively, he brightened and turned to his assistant.

"Well, Tiger," he said quite cheerily, "I suppose you'll want to go to the funeral. Okay, now, Captain Starr, let's pick up all of our loose ends. Just where does the case stand now?"

"Say, John," interrupted Tiger, "Frank and I sort of feel that there is some number one man, a big shot, in this somewhere—"

"No, Tiger!" Francis cut in sharply. He looked meaningfully at Captain Starr. "I think that we were wrong there. I feel now that Buster master-minded the whole deal, except for the narcotics; and that was Cannelli's tie-in. What do you think, Captain Starr? Or has Cannelli given you anyone else?"

"No, Joe is pleading guilty to a narcotics charge. They're federal anyway. But he will not implicate anyone else. That's definite. I, er, had a talk with him."

"Possibly there's no one else to be implicated, like Frank says; but still, I sort of thought for awhile there . . ." remarked Olsen.

Captain Starr rose from his chair.

"I guess this washes up our three murders, then. This pretty much ties it all up with Buster, and the department is closing the cases on that note."

Tiger laughed shortly. "It was lucky that we got ourselves out of there before the building went down! Have you seen it since, John?"

"Yes, I drove out by there this morning. The whole place was pretty old, and the wood was dry. It went pretty fast."

"I suppose so. Lucky that no one except Buster got hurt."

"Yes," said Starr. The police now feel that he must have been trapped up there in his office and either fell or deliberately jumped from that window. The fire department thinks that the fire started in some loose photographic equipment, chemicals or something. It's hard to tell, there's so little left of the building. Morley, I, er, suppose that the department owes the Agency some considerable thanks. Er, unofficially, of course. And you know that you have mine—for everything. You men managed a good police job on this. And—well, thanks!"

Tiger grinned, "I told you, John."

Starr flushed, then added, "I'll admit, Morley, if Olsen hadn't convinced me that you were okay, we wouldn't even have got started on this. I had some ideas. Well, I admit that I was probably wrong."

Francis, now also standing, put one hand on his hip and smoothed his wavy hair with the other in an unmistakable gesture as he gushed,

"Oh, Captain Starr! I bet you tell that to all the boys . . ."

The police officer strode to the door, shaking his head. There he turned and glared at Tiger.

"I just don't get it . . ."

The officer, hand on the door, was about to leave when in a more serious tone Francis stopped him. He paused, turning his head.

"Captain, you'd better take it easy in the future when giving medicine to sick dogs. You might get more seriously bitten."

The detective's eyes dropped to his bandaged hand. Then he looked at Francis. Turning so as to include Tiger, he said, "See you men around." He went out, closing the door gently behind him.

During this last, Tiger had picked up the discarded newspaper. After a wave of the hand at the departing Starr, he remarked, "I always read this guy Karl. Say, have you seen his column yet, Frank?"

"Nope! Been too busy. Think I'll have a workout at the gym this afternoon. What about you?"

Tiger had been reading the paper and now looked up angrily.

156

"Say, I don't think I like this."

"What."

"Oh, it's Bert. Bert Karl. He's kidding people all the time. But this is kinda snotty . . ."

He passed the paper back to Francis, who quickly found Karl's column. About in the middle of it, he read:

Friday Fritata:

> 'that old gang of mine'. Only last Monday we all gathered around the big table in Flanagan's Back Room. Senator Bruce Martin, Captain John Starr (of the police stars—get it?), Joe Cannelli, the restaurateur, Tiger Olsen, the ex-Marine and late car salesman, and myself! We all laughed merrily at some mention of the gay set, including one of Joe's employees, and also about a new member of our local swish set who has inherited a detective agency. Joe was unrefined! Today, the papers headline the tragic death of kindly Senator Martin, long the City's leading citizen. He was found, shortly after death, by his old friend Captain Starr, who, peculiarly, had gone to tell him of the astounding arrest of Joe Cannelli as a drug dealer. Also noted: the ex-Marine, ex-MAN-about town Tiger Olsen, has gone to work for the ex-chorus boy who is now a detective! And, worse and worse, girls, though there seems to be no connection, the Baths have burned down! Whatta week!

Francis read through this and laughed whole-heartedly, but Tiger was still annoyed.

"Hell, Frank! Bert and I have been pretty good friends, and this is kinda nasty."

"Well, dearie, you've got broad shoulders. Don't let it worry you. It's all in fun. Just the same, that one better not let me catch her with her hair down . . ."

Tiger shook his head: "Uh-uh, Frank. I don't think he's . . ."

"Huh!" snorted Frank. "I always say that anyone knowing that much of the words and music is bound to have done the dance routines too! By the way, I forgot . . ." Francis pulled some money from a pocket and laid several large bills on the desk. "And, another thing I'm always saying is something about not looking at either end of gift horses. Anyway, we got a sort of cash bonus on this deal. If your conscience doesn't bother you any more than mine, you'll pick up your share."

Hesitantly, Olsen drew the money towards himself, then picked it up and pocketed it, with a slightly questioning look at his employer.

"Just let's say that I found it in the fire. If I hadn't picked it up, it would have gone up in smoke. And I don't think that any living soul has a claim on it. Satisfy you?"

After a moment, Tiger matched Francis' smile with one of his own.

"Whatta job! And whatta boss! Eh, Boss?"

At this moment, a disturbance in the outer office was clearly evident. Both men turned that way as the door flew open and in stalked a very agitated and slightly disheveled elderly lady bearing a traveling pet-cage. This she set down roughly on Francis' desk. Then, fixing him with a beady eye, she declared,

"You, sir, are a charleton!"

"Ah, yes, and a bright good morning—or is it now afternoon—to you, too, Mrs. Bagnold.

"This beast that you foisted off on me is not the Emir of Afghanistan." Turning on Tiger, she included him in her wrath. "And you, sir! You should be ashamed! Introducing this—this fiend into my innocent household."

"Well, madam," pleaded Olsen, "I was almost positively sure from your description that this was your pet. Are you very sure? That is—"

"Yes, Mrs. Bagnold," offered Francis. "You did say they all looked something alike. Perhaps he's just upset, being away from his home and all those—"

"Mr. Morley! Let's have no more of this gross deception. This is not the animal my sister sent to me—the Emir. And I am quite sure of it! Her reason for sending the Emir was that she thought he should have a change of surroundings after his operation. For two days and nights now, this beast and my three poor innocent Persians have made my home a shambles—until we were finally able to catch this monster! Believe me, gentlemen, this is not the Emir. He has very definitely never been operated on."

Tiger hid his face in his handkerchief with a burst of spurious coughing. Francis just managed to restrain his mirth as he replied with dignity, "Madame", he said, "if there has been an error, my secretary will give you a check in full refund of your fee."

For a moment, the austere dowager allowed a look of kindly reminiscence to show on her face.

"That won't be necessary, young man. The, er, display was, er, interesting! However, should my darlings, er, conceive as a result of this unprincipled feline's aggressiveness, I shall seriously consider naming you in a paternity suit."

With this she stalked to the door, where she paused. Turning back, she added with a sigh, "Truly, it was magnificent. Believe me! All three in one afternoon! I just want to be sure that you will take good care of this over-energetic beast. I do realize that it was all a mistake. But, well, at my age, it's just too much! Good day, gentlemen —and you too, you thing!"

With this Mrs. Bagnold flounced out. Hattie came in to find Francis and Tiger limp with laughter.

The cat in the cage paused in washing its wise face to eye this new female.

"Well, Mr. Morley, and what do we do with it?" demanded Hattie.

Catching his breath, Francis roared,

"Get her! Call him Butch and put him on the payroll. After all, we need some live pussy around this office."

Butch said, "mmrrroww!"

THE END